IMAGINE THAT

JAMES AGEE JR.   KATIE JOHNS   TED GARCIA
LORRAINE BRADNER

Treasure Ink Press

Cover Design: James Agee Jr.

Editor: Lindsey Meadows

ISBN: 9798748263450

CONTENTS

history while she spends new year's grounded and has to write an essay on the 1920's for her English class. Dozing off before 2020, she wakes up in the early twentieth century and makes a vaguely familiar friend for the day who helps her see that the era is not as bad as it seems.

Aunt Charlotte of Sheffield by Ted Garcia

Daniel is not excited when his mother forces him to spend part of the summer with his snobby aunt in her ritzy beach community. Things quickly take a turn during their visit when Daniel discovers that his Aunt Charlotte is keeping a secret. It challenges Daniel's idea of reality and if discovered could put himself and his family in jeopardy.

The Heart Healer by Lorraine Bradner

To everyone else, Lily was just a normal fifteen-year-old girl whose parents were genius scientists. Unbeknownst to others, Lily was a cardiac patient who suffered from anxiety and was going to require surgery to live. As her condition worsened, she struggled through isolation as others began to see her non-normal side and avoided her. Lily was alone and scared until one fateful day she came across a dog that changed everything. Join Lily in her journey to freedom as she undergoes a strange adventure that ends up changing the lives of millions.

MY WORLD

Finch has always known that his mother doesn't care for him. Things take a turn for the worse when they are banished from the only community that he has ever known. With only himself to rely on, it is a matter of life and death.

MY WORLD

By James Agee Jr.

My world changed one evening, as night fell and stamped out the remnants of all that was light. The fireplace crackled in the hearth and was the only warm thing for miles. Our house was nothing more than a pile of bricks that had hastily been built about fifty years ago. The walls were slick with mold and mildew and the windows so covered in filth that I could scarcely ever see out of them. Still, I would find myself longing to be back there, not for the comfort, because there was none, rather I would miss a time when my life was more mine.

Mother sits in a rickety rocking chair, the fire casting her in a wicked glow. She turns and looks at me every so often with a hollow gaze. She is holding a clay pot, the lid of which she removed hours ago. Inside of that clay pot are the ashes of my father. She slowly dips her hand into the pot and lets it rest there a few moments before removing it and rubbing the ashes between her fingers. I find this to be a repulsive act but she has done it every evening since she obtained the pot of ashes.

Sometimes she whispers words that I cannot make out, speaking to my father. I doubt that he would want to hear her voice again, I doubt that he would want to hear anything that she has to say. She was a cruel wife and an even worse mother.

My mother's name is etched into my mind for all eternity. As a child I was made to sit in an uncomfortable wooden chair and write her name over and over until my fingers bled from the sores created by the rudimentary pencil. I would write it for hours on tear stained pages until there would be no more room left.

"Canyon." I find myself mouthing the name.

Our community is small and those of us who live here are given simple names at birth. Canyon once told me during a lesson that there are some places where people have more than one name, but we do not ever go to those places. If we were to ever leave the community then we would never be allowed to return. My own name is not so special as hers and I didn't learn to spell it until after I had mastered spelling the letters C-A-N-Y-O-N.

My name is Finch, like the bird. I have never actually

seen a finch in real life because there aren't many animals here, but Canyon has told me that they are a perfectly adequate bird.

"They are nothing special, but they are also not dreadful. They are perfectly adequate. Just as you are, my child." She told me.

I am thankful that my lessons ended many moons ago. When I reached my thirteenth year Canyon stopped teaching me about the world.

"Why are my lessons stopping?" I recall asking.

"Because you know all that there is to know about the world now. There is no need for lessons anymore." She said.

I do not feel as if I know everything there is to know, but if Canyon says that it is true then it must be so. The flickering embers dance shadows upon her aged face. She turns to look at me again and I am unsure if I can meet her gaze. Sometimes I am afraid of her, but perhaps that is the way it is supposed to be. Maybe everyone is afraid of their mothers.

She reaches her hand into the pot of ashes and pulls out a handful of the sandlike remains of my father. She holds the fistful of ashes inches above the pot and slowly lets the ashes fall back to their resting place. My insides feel like ice, like cold electricity is flowing through my veins. I want to take the pot of ashes from her and hide it away somewhere that she will never be able to find it, but I know that is impossible. I am not brave enough to do something like that and even if I were, Canyon knows everything that there is to know about this place and would find them in no time.

I shut my eyes and breath in steady breaths. I count them to myself so that my focus is on something other than the incessant rocking of the chair and Canyon's knowing smile as she handles my father's ashes. He couldn't stand her and I believe that she knew it. Now, at least in this small room, she has him where he can never leave.

One. I breathe in a deep breath and push aside my feelings of anger.

Two. I breathe out, letting my worries dissipate.

Three. There is a loud knock at the door, so loud that I worry the barrier will not hold.

I open my eyes and expect to see a look of shock on Canyon's face, but instead she rocks in the chair as if there is not anyone at the door.

"Open. The. Door." She says to me, accentuating each word with meaning so that I know not to disobey her command.

I quickly push myself up from the floor where I was sitting in the corner of the room. I am not allowed near the fire because Canyon says I soak up all of the warmth and leave none for her. I reach for the brass handle of the door and turn it. The door swings wildly open and a group of men from our community barge in. Their boots leave outlines of mud on the floorboards.

"Canyon, it is time." One of the men says to her.

I look to my mother in the hopes that she understands more about what is happening than I do. She stands up slowly and returns the lid to the pot of ashes. She walks over to me and wipes her hands clean on my shirt, smudges of ash embedding themselves into the cloth.

"You can keep him if you would like." She says, looking to me and then to the men.

The ice in my veins runs colder and a spark of anger flares in my chest once more.

"Enough nonsense, your son would be as useless to us as he is to you. We don't need the burden of another mouth to feed."

Canyon walks over to a burlap sack in the corner of the room and hefts it over her shoulder. She places the pot of ashes into a large pocket on her shawl and the weight of it hangs heavy.

"Finch! Come on. We're leaving." She commands.

The men step aside and let her walk past. She exits the house, seemingly not caring if I am following behind. One of the men motions for me to leave too. I look to the fire still crackling in the hearth, sustained by a single log, and figure that I must go with her. I have no place amongst my community. If it hadn't been for Canyon, I would have been made to leave long before now.

As I pass under the doorframe one of the men, my father's best friend, places a hand on my shoulder and says, "This was his dying wish."

He must mean my father. I cannot fathom why my father would have wanted Canyon and I to leave our house and the community. Canyon walks along ahead, the sack of belongings rattling at her back. I wonder why she didn't tell me if she knew. I would have liked to have packed some of my belongings as well, as meager and few as they are.

Canyon has never given me much thought beyond being a presence she could not be rid of. Her pace quickens and I know that if I do not try and move quicker she will leave me behind and be all the happier for it. I am her burden, I always have been, but how heavy of a burden can a single finch be?

Canyon moves with a quick pace, one that I can scarcely keep up with. My legs are tired and I have not eaten since the last sunset. Canyon had a meal of dried fish and bread. When I asked her for some she spit on the ground and replied, "You should have brought your own."

The gnawing sensation in my stomach urges me to find food, but I cannot when there is so much else to think of. There are very few animals in these woods, so even if I did try and capture something for sustenance I could only hope to get a malnourished rabbit. These woods were not meant to provide life to those who inhabit it.

Canyon has a defiant brilliance to her that I have no doubt could outlast even the trees themselves, but I have doubts about myself. My feet are wrapped in a thin cloth that has been pierced through by the jagged rocks that protrude from the ground. Trickles of blood appear, but I push the notion of pain away. Weakness is not to be shown around Canyon.

The sun is high in the sky once more and I wonder at how far we have come. Even if I wanted to run back to the crumbling brick house, would I be able to find my way? The community will have likely given it as residence to a new family by now. The community does not waste.

Canyon stops abruptly and I almost run into her. She points to a patch of berries hidden amidst the briars.

"There you go. Eat some of those if you're so hungry." She says with the hint of something sinister in her voice.

I kneel down and reach for one of the berries and my hand catches on one of the briars. A burst of bright red blood emerges from the small wound and I feel faint for a moment. I pick one of the berries and hold it up to examine.

"It's poisonous." I say.

Canyon looks at me, "I know."

She laughs and walks on, not caring if I follow. Some part of me wants to diverge from her path and go a different way. Another part of me wants to sneak some of these berries into her food supply. The part of me that wins, is the part that follows close behind and says nothing aloud.

Night falls and I expect it to be my last. My hunger has deepened so that I can hardly stand upright. Canyon builds a small fire and cooks a stew of herbs and dried meats that she pulls from the burlap sack. It would have been so simple for her to tell me in advance that we would be removed from the community and to have allowed me to pack some things of my own.

My eyes blur with the smoke from the fire and I listen for something...anything...but the only sounds I hear are those of Canyon rustling in the bag for ingredients for her stew.

"Please Canyon, I will die if I do not get something to eat." I plead with her.

She smiles, "You should have brought some food of

your own. It wouldn't be fair for both of us to starve, now would it?" She asks.

I do not reply, rather I fix my gaze on the fire. Between the flickers I imagine that I see her take a pinch of the ashes from the pot and place them in her stew, but when I try and focus my blurring vision she is simply stirring the stew with a stick.

If I had more anger inside of me, perhaps I could say something powerful enough to change her mind, but anger has never brought words of wisdom and I cannot imagine that it would start now. Canyon stops stirring the stew, "Finch."

"Yes." I say, hopeful that she will offer me some of the stew.

"Remember what we've talked about? You're soaking up all of the warmth from the fire. Move away, you wouldn't want your mother to freeze to death."

Something in my breaks and I feel a flood of tears stream down my dirt covered face. I will them to stop, but they keep flowing with all of the hurt inside of me. I muster as much strength as I can and half-walk, half-crawl, my way away from the fire until I am sitting against a tree out of view from Canyon. The only sign that I am not alone is the smell wafting from the stew and the smoke of the fire that winds its way through the branches of the trees.

Moonlight illuminates the forest in a full gray-blue that I cannot help but think of as beautiful. My eyes are heavy with sleep, but the pain in my stomach keeps me from finding rest. Occasionally, I will hear Canyon humming a happy tune between mouthfuls of her stew.

I notice the sensation of a hand on my shoulder. I do not know how long it has been there. I turn my head slightly and expect to see Canyon, but instead I make out a blurry figure who looks to be about my age. There is a moment where I wonder if it is real or if it is a hallucination. The figure squeezes my shoulder and then dissipates into the air.

Who was that?

What was that?

I catch movement out of the corner of my eye near a large tree and see two hazy figures walking side by side until they are gone. My hand feels a patch of berries beside of the tree that I rest against. I don't even care if they are poisonous, I have to eat something. I fill my stomach with the berries and as the hunger fades, so does a portion of my sorrow.

THOSE WHO DWELL

I awake to the sound of leaves rustling in the morning breeze. Some of my strength has returned from my meal of berries last night, enough that I feel capable of another day's journey. I make my way to the small clearing where Canyon was last night. She is asleep with her arms wrapped around the pot of ashes. The burlap sack of supplies is beside of her.

For a moment I consider taking the supplies and leaving her to fend for herself. She is no doubt better at surviving than I am. I step closer, feeling light on my feet, but when she stirs I am startled and rush behind a nearby tree. I expect to feel my pulse racing and my heart pounding in my chest, but instead I feel nothing at all.

I cannot continue this journey with Canyon, my mother. I try to think of the good things that she has done for me, but the list is extremely short. My memories are tinged with pain and heartache as I try my best to recall them. She taught me lessons about life and she taught me lessons about surviving, and for that I will allow myself to be grateful.

I suppose that I was always envious of the idea of having a mother that loved me, but I was always thankful that my father did. I consider going for the pot of ashes and taking them with me, just to get them away from her, but I cannot muster the courage to do it. It hurts knowing that my father's remains will be with her forever.

Suddenly I feel as if I am being watched. I look in the distance and make out the figure of a person. Perhaps my mind was not playing tricks on me last night. Before I can even think about what to do, my feet are moving at a swift pace towards the figure. I almost expect the person to run from me, but they remain still and unmoving. The berries were not poisonous, In fact, I feel better than I have in a long time.

I finally reach the figure and see that it is someone wearing what seems to be a mask. A brown cloak hangs from their shoulders.

"Are you lost?" The figure asks me.

I can tell by their tone that they are a man, perhaps one of the community members who has come to check on us.

"Are you from the community?" I ask in reply.

"No. I asked you if you are lost."

"I don't think so. I don't know where I am or where I am going, but I don't think that means that I am lost."

"You can come with me if you would like."

I look at the figure shrouded in mystery. Though I know nothing about this person, when I consider going back to Canyon there is not much of a choice to make.

"I will come with you." I say.

The figure nods and then motions for me to follow alongside them. I wonder if Canyon will miss me or even notice that I am no longer there. My thoughts are answered when a few moments later I hear a thunderous cry from the direction that I came.

"Finch!" Canyon's voice booms through the trees.

I fear what she will do if she finds me. This is an awfully large forest and this stranger seems to know where we are going, so my hope is that I will not ever see Canyon again.

I follow the stranger and wonder at how I was finally able to break free from Canyon. I had imagined that I would be stuck with her for the rest of my life. Though she never wanted me, I didn't think I ever had a choice but to follow her.

We walk along, the ground beneath me feeling lighter with every step, until we reach a path made of smooth pebbles. I step towards the path, but the stranger holds out their arm and stops me.

"You must learn to see properly." The stranger says.

There is such certainty in their voice that I question myself for a moment.

Do I not see properly already?

I am not entirely sure what the stranger means by their statement, but it is clear that I am not allowed to step on the path until I figure it out. The stranger grabs my wrist and stars pulling me in another direction. Panic floods my body and I worry that I have made a terrible mistake by coming with the stranger.

The stranger pulls me along in the new direction until I am willingly following and then releases my arm. A cave looms beneath a cliff-face and I hope that we are not going there. Nothing good ever happens inside of caves. The community warned the children to never go near one. I always felt lucky enough to never have seen a cave in person. Now, with the grand opening beckoning us forward I understand why we were warned.

A bat screeches above as it flies from the mouth of the cave and into the evening. Soon night will have fallen and we will be surrounded by darkness.

"We should stop and build a fire." I say.

The stranger ignores me and keeps walking towards the cave. I could turn and run, leave this cave and the stranger behind, but where would I go? Even if I wanted to find my way back to Canyon, I don't think that I ever could. The forest is so vast and confusing, every tree looks the same as the last.

At the cave entrance I feel cool air surround me. More bats are emerging for their nightly flight. I have never seen one of these creatures in person before now, but Canyon warned me about them.

"Bats are dangerous, just like most creatures." She told me on a day when my lessons focused on learning about new creatures.

There are so many animals that I know about, yet have never actually seen. I only know that these creatures are bats because of the few characteristics that I learned from Canyon.

A bat lands on the strangers shoulder and for a moment I worry that it will bite them. The stranger turns to me and the bat leaps from their shoulder to my chest. My heart races and I fear that the creature can hear my pulse.

"Close your eyes." The stranger instructs me.

"How can I?" I ask, the fear evident in my voice.

"Close your eyes." The stranger repeats.

I do as I am told and close my eyes. The dark world around me becomes even darker until I am consumed by nothingness.

"Open your eyes and see." I hear the stranger say.

I do as I am told, but instead of seeing the dark night that I expect, the world is illuminated. I look at my hands and feet and see that I am still me. Nothing about me has changed except for my vision. The bat on my chest leaps off and into the air where it flaps its wings and flies off into the night. My vision jerks away abruptly and I understand that I am seeing what the bat sees.

Though I do not completely understand what is happening to me, I feel weightless and free in a way that I never have. I do not worry about what is to come next, I simply open my eyes and see the world in an entirely new way.

SIX

SIGHT

t first my vision is hard to focus, but after a few minutes I am able to see things that I never knew possible. I know that there are insects inside of the trees and how far I am from each one of them. I know things that I never did before.

The clouds are not what I had expected them to be. When I go through a cloud it is as if it were nothing more than a vapor, I had expected them to have more... substance. I feel as if I could see the world from this vantage point forever and be happy.

A bright flicker of something catches the bats attention and I see that we are immediately propelled downward towards it. The closer we get I start to realize that it is a campfire. My heart starts to race because I know exactly whose campfire it is.

25

Canyon sits close to the flame and holds the pot of my father's ashes. I am nearby, perhaps on a branch of a tree. She does not seem to notice my presence. Something shiny glimmers on her face and I realize that it is a tear. A steady stream of tears falls from her eyes. Much of her tears land in the ashes where they seem to spark some sort of reaction. Perhaps it is my newfound vision that allows me to see the glow of color that her tears make when they land upon the ashes, or perhaps it is only my imagination.

She sits the ashes beside of her and wipes the back of her palms across her nose. I do not believe that she is crying for me. After the life that I had with her, it isn't possible that she would care that I am gone. If she isn't crying for me, then what is she crying about?

Her mouth moves and a mumbling of words comes out, "I never wanted to be like this. I never wanted this..."

She does not appear to be talking to anyone in particular. She repeats those words to herself and rocks gently towards the fire. I hope that she has enough warmth now. At least she no longer has to worry that I am stealing the warmth from her.

The bat makes a loud screeching sound and it startles her. She looks up at the bat, at me, and it looks as if she might hurdle something my way, but instead the tension in her face eases and she continues to cry.

I feel a jolt in my chest and in an instant I am seeing through my own eyes once again.

"What just happened?" I ask.

The stranger looks to me and says, "You finally learned to see."

SEVEN

FOLLOWING

The stranger leads me back to the pebble path. As the sun rises I notice the subtle colors that reflect in the smooth stones. I want to reach down and pick one of the stones up, to keep it in my pocket, but some part of me won't allow it.

The stranger steps gently onto the path and motions for me to follow. I look ahead and try to make out our destination. There must be something marvelous up ahead, but I cannot see it. Branches of trees block my view of whatever it is we are walking towards. Though I cannot see where I am going, I feel in my heart that it will be worth the journey.

We walk for what feels like a small eternity, and somehow it also feels like we have just started. Time has lost all meaning and I do not regret losing it. I notice a boy leaning up against a tree nearby. I don't want to step off of the path for fear that I would not be able to get back on, but I do pause for a moment and take a closer look.

"Do you know him?" The stranger asks.

I puzzle over where I have seen him before. I know that he is familiar in some way, but I cannot pinpoint how. The stranger steps gingerly off of the path and walks over to the boy. The boy's eyes are fluttering open and closed. I feel that he is exhausted.

The stranger places their hand on his shoulder and the memory comes flooding back to me. I am that boy. The night that I met the stranger, that is what I am witnessing now. I expect the boy...me...to get up and join us on the path, but he doesn't. He sits by the tree and watches as the stranger joins me on the path.

The stranger takes off his hood and I see for the first time another face that I recognize. The face of my father stares at me. Whatever worries I had before are now completely gone. He nods at me, knowing that I am with him now, as he has always been with me.

I have so many questions, but none of them seem important anymore. I look to the boy by the tree, his eyes closed and a handful of berries resting limply at his side. Whoever he was, he is no more. I nod back at my father, both of us knowing that this is something new and wonderful. We walk side-by-side towards whatever lies ahead.

ABOUT JAMES AGEE JR.

James Agee Jr. is the author of multiple young adult and children's novels. His books offer a variety of stories so that all readers are able to find one of his works to can enjoy.

LIVING HISTORY

Those who fail to learn the past are doomed to repeat it, right? Sophie Westin experiences what they say about history while she spends new year's grounded and has to write an essay on the 1920's for her English class. Dozing off before 2020, she wakes up in the early twentieth century and makes a vaguely familiar friend for the day who helps her see that the era is not as bad as it seems.

LIVING HISTORY

By Katie Johns

ONE

LIVING HISTORY

Sophie A. Westin could not believe she was grounded over New Year's. This was a consequence of potentially failing her English class. Now she had to spend the evening writing an essay while her friends celebrated. The assignment was given ahead of a unit studying turn-of-the-century stories like *The Secret Garden*, *The Metamorphosis*, and *Ethan Frome*. So its topic was to discuss what life was like one hundred years ago.

"As if Shakespeare and *Pride and Prejudice* weren't far enough in history." Sophie sneered at the thought of more centuries-old literature to stagger through. In her mind, some of those dusty old stories turned into films for a reason. She especially enjoyed the action and zombie elements added to the Jane Austen work that came out a few years ago. But she'd rather be one of the undead than sit and read old stuff in any format. Not in print, not an audio recording, not even on an electronic device. Reading and writing weren't difficult for her as much as they weren't her favorite things to do. In some way or another, she managed to skirt by with a bare minimum of her classwork for half the year. Her "helicopter parents" finally caught her evasions when they checked the online grade postings and held a conference with her teacher. All leading to her being home at 11:45 pm on New Year's Eve 2019, staring at a blank word document on the computer screen instead of watching the ball drop with her friends.

"One hundred years ago was the Stone Age." She started typing. "Coming right after when dinosaurs were wiped out, but before anybody had electricity, cell phones, cars, and the internet."

"Nineteen-twenty seems so boring!" The thought only added to her indifference. But a fun spring break was on the line if she didn't apply herself and bring up her grades. After some deliberation, she had to start again. She held down the backspace button and watched the cursor eat the product of her bad mood.

"*Downton Abbey* wasn't right after the Stone Age anyways." She corrected her train of thought using one of the few pop culture references she knew related to the previous century. She stretched out of her desk chair and got up to lay across her bed and think of another way to start. "Maybe something will come to me in a dream." She mused and yawned as she sunk into her cushy comforter. "All the best stuff does, right?" The next thing she knew her eyes would not stay open, her breath deepened, and she rolled over onto her side to sleep.

Meanwhile, sixteen-year-old Winnie Brady rang in the new year, as the flapper she always wanted to be, drinking and dancing at clubs around the city. Hopping parties were all over during the holidays, so in the wee hours of the new year, Winnie and her Aunt Molly finally made it back to their apartment. After hitting the sack for a few hours, they awoke late in the morning to make some coffee and breakfast. With the food nearly ready, Winnie turned from the kitchen to set the dining table when she noticed a strange person awaking on their rollaway bed in the living room.

"Good morning," Winnie curiously greeted their visitor, then nudged her aunt to draw her attention as well.

"Morning," Sophie yawned, stretching and rubbing her eyes.

"Forgive me if I'm too frank, dear," Winnie asked, "but I don't remember you even coming home with us last night."

"Where am I?" Even through her sleepy haze, Sophie was immediately confused. "I'm certain I never even left home last night! I'm grounded! I need to call my mom!" In her growing fret, she started feeling and looking around on the bed and checking the floor nearby for her phone.

"You're on Chesterton Street," Aunt Molly replied as she delivered the hot food from the stove to the table, supposing Sophie was just from another part of town. "If she's in the city, you're welcome to use our telephone." She gestured to a black box on the wall. "Would you like some breakfast before you go?"

That was no help to Sophie though. Her town did not have a Chesterton Street. She didn't know where she was, who she was with, or much less where her own phone was. The offer for breakfast didn't even register with her at first. Knowledge told her that that thing on the wall was a telephone, but what was mortifying was that she did not know how to use a phone like that, or much less did she know anybody's phone number from memory.

Deflated and distressed, she shuffled to the table. "I don't know where I am, where to go, or what to do!" Sophie finally muttered a response, taking a seat. Molly and Winnie were concerned about the well-being of this strange girl sitting with them.

"We'll help you out as much as we can, dear," Aunt Molly consoled. "Maybe something in your stomach will help you think more clearly?" Sophie dolefully obliged.

"Hot dog, though!" Winnie quietly laughed as they

ate, " You seem a lot like me, sneaking out when you're grounded! And on New Year's, of all times!"

Perplexed, Sophie looked at Winnie for clarification. She never met this woman before in her life as far as she was concerned.

"I rarely did what anybody wanted me to do growing up in Ferris Creek!" Winnie boasted, "Plus, nights like last night would be unthinkable! If the blue rinse brigade there had their way, I would've been a stuffy, settled-down sap with a couple of babies right now. They never cared for the city styles anyways, but they started thinking the worst of me after they caught me leaving the store with rouge and a radical fashion magazine. So, my parents sent me to live here with Aunt Molly. She lost her husband in The Great War and moved here to start her life over."

Sophie was politely intrigued, if not a little enviously wishing she could move away from her parents. As she listened to Winnie, something started to seem a hint familiar about her, but she couldn't quite put her finger on it.

"I'll go to the news stand after breakfast," Winnie announced as they finished eating. "I bet the fresh air would do some good too if you'd like to come along." Sophie agreed.

The women cleared their plates, and borrowing some of their outerwear, Sophie accompanied Winnie on her errand. If nothing else, she determined she was in an apartment complex somewhere. Where exactly she had no clue and was more confused the second she stepped outside. Black Model T's cruised the streets and a skyscraper in construction stretched the skyline. Every pedestrian she saw was dressed sharp and wore a hat. A few men even tipped theirs to her. She was mystified, but couldn't let it keep her still though as she didn't want to lose Winnie in the bustling crowds. She caught up to her in front of an appliance store. The advertising in the window displayed its wares as "new", "better", "afford-able", and 'modern", but some of them were strange to her.

"What's all this?" Sophie asked Winnie.

"Why, that's a radio and some of its components," Winnie pointed to each item as she answered, "A popcorn maker, an electric toaster...and lightbulbs. I'm glad we stopped; I need to get some."

After Winnie's side-trip into the store, they crossed a couple street intersections. Not a traffic light in sight, Sophie noticed. Winnie was one of few who practiced caution when crossing, but others--pedestrian and driver alike-- didn't seem to think as much of it. At one point, Sophie wasn't sure which scared her more: the fact she was nowhere remotely close to home or watching children flirt with traffic.

However, she felt close to losing her mind when they

arrived at their destination. Perusing the covers and front pages while Winnie made her selections, she noticed they were dated 1920-something. Sophie Westin wasn't just away from home; she was out of her own time! Immediately, she racked her brain trying to remember anything she learned about the 1920's. *"Has the Spanish flu happened yet? Where's Al Capone and the gangsters? Is* Annie *set in this time period? Would I be an orphan? I'm not even born yet!..."* She could kick herself for not paying better attention in class.

"My dear, you look like you've seen a ghost!" Winnie startled her out of her spinning thoughts when she turned to her.

"Maybe just...too much air..." Sophie tried to brush off.

"I'll have to brew you some tea when we get back home," Winnie put her arm around Sophie and they made their return to the apartment. As they walked back, that vague sense of Sophie's familiarity with Winnie returned. She caught a faint whiff of her perfume as she was drawn close but didn't know why she recognized it. She looked like someone she knew personally too, not just someone she saw in some random textbook photo or something.

Before they even got back inside, the two of them heard music blaring from down their hallway. Aunt Molly liked to play the records or radio loud when no one else was home.

"Turn it off, Aunt Molly!" Winnie shouted as they came through the door. "Sophie may be getting worse!" Aunt Molly quieted the record player, and ushered Sophie to a seat in the living room while Winnie began the tea.

"Oh, it wasn't bothering me," Sophie admitted. "I actually really liked it!" Whatever was just on didn't sound like every other song to her; the swing and sway of jazz sounded unique and truly fun. For the first time all day, Sophie seemed less blanched too.

"Alright," Aunt Molly conceded to turning the music back on. "But I'll set the volume lower just in case. Just take it easy for a while but let us know if you're feeling bad again, ok?"

Sophie nodded and settled into the chair. Aunt Molly draped a blanket across her lap before restarting the music player. A couple minutes later, Winnie handed her a hot brew and the two women settled into the sofa across from her to read over the publications that were picked up earlier. Sophie started to find herself at ease as she sipped her drink. Apart from the music and an occasional conversation about something the women were reading, the silence was comfortable. *Just need a movie on and this is the perfect day*, Sophie thought.

"Could we visit Florida this summer, Aunt Molly?" Winnie asked over her magazine. "It's sounding like a swell place to visit and I could work on getting a suntan!"

Eventually, the telephone rang through the quiet. Winnie rose to answer it.

"Hello?...Oh, hi, Ben! Happy New Year to you too, thank you!...Well, I'd love to, but would you please hold for a moment?" She turned to Sophie, "Do you feel up for a movie, dear?"

"Absolutely!" As if she read her mind.

Winnie turned back to the phone, "So, listen...I have a friend over and I don't want her to feel left out. How does a group date sound? Super! I'll see you later!"

"That was Ben inviting me to a movie," Winnie told her curious aunt after hanging up.

"Ben from the sandwich shop?" Aunt Molly clarified, "What happened to Tony?"

"Tony is playing at the Empire Club across town tonight. I was going to go if nothing else was going on."

"That Edwin fellow from the sports club seemed nice. What happened to him?"

"I'm old news to him. He's goofy about Della Stanton this week, who's a ritzy bore if you ask me..."

The two women paused in thought for a moment, deciding who else to invite. Meanwhile, Sophie was starting to see how she and Winnie could be alike, listening to her talk about boys, style, vacations, and getting in trouble.

"I could see if Timothy is available," Picking the phone back up, the idea finally came to invite her co-worker. "He's a good sort." When the matter of gathering friends settled, Winnie looked over Sophie to size up another one.

"Are you sure you're interested?" Winnie asked again.

"Of course!" Sophie reaffirmed. "I'm really not sick."

"No doubt about that, honey. I'm just not sure your current glad rags agree…"

"Oh," Sophie looked down at her mismatched socks, thinning flannel sleep pants, and well-worn hoodie missing its drawstring. Her hair topped her head in a messy bundle that needed washed. "Right! We're going on a date!" She chuckled. "This isn't my go-to outfit, I swear!"

"I think you're about the right size to wear some of my things. Let's glam you up a bit." Winnie led Sophie to her wardrobe. Accustomed to its black-and-white portrayals in her own time, Sophie felt surreal seeing everything from the decade in color, much less its fashion. Lush texture and vibrant color filled Winnie's closet, namely as dresses and gowns. The two played dress-up until Sophie settled on a black blue, silk satin dress topped with a white taffeta, gold-beaded caplet and a fashionably uneven hemline that covered her knees. She never wore many loose-fitting dresses and wearing rayon stockings were new to her. Nonetheless, she thought the dress was breathtaking on her. Winnie worked Sophie's hair into a faux bob, so her longer hair didn't hide the pattern on her shoulders. Winnie wore a flowery Robe de Style and touched up her short hairline with a side part and curls. Sophie thought she looked cute.

A few hours later, they were at the movie house; Sophie with Timothy, Winnie with Ben, and a slew of their other dating friends. Judging by the rest of the group's talk, the "talkies" were becoming a new thing, whereas Sophie had never even sat through a whole black-and-white film before then, but she still enjoyed it. Afterwards, they went for root beer and ice cream before visiting the Empire Club to listen to Tony and his band. The rest of the group taught Sophie some of the popular dance moves, like the Charleston and foxtrot. At that point, Sophie was having a blast, nearly forgetting how boring she originally thought the 1920's were.

At some odd hour of the morning, the group date exited the club, each couple going their own way until Winnie, Ben, Sophie, and Timothy remained. Winnie and Ben started to get rather affectionate with each other, so Timothy and Sophie wandered down the street to give them some space. Sophie didn't want to cut in, but she also didn't want to leave without Winnie; she would've gotten herself lost trying to get back to the apartment on her own.

Sophie found Timothy really was a good sport and almost hated that she couldn't guarantee spending more time with him. He was a fun dance teacher and partner. He was a college student, studying economics and business. Leaving Ben and Winnie to their lip-locking, Sophie politely listened to him talk about stock prices and margins. Sophie couldn't quite remember what that had to do with the decade, though.

"...if the market doesn't start taking margin calls more seriously, a lot of the economic sector could be in big trouble soon..." was the last thing Sophie heard him say before some shadow clutched her from behind and carried her away, struggling and trying to scream. The shadow lured her back into the alley it came from where a few more shadows bound her up and forced her into the back of a delivery vehicle. A couple more bodies followed her, but she couldn't tell who.

When Sophie regained her senses, they were being unloaded from the vehicle by gangsters! They had brought them to an ominous warehouse holding barrels and crates of alcohol.

"Reg! This ain't the mayor's daughter!" She heard one of them spit as they lifted her from the cargo space. "Can't you do nothin' right?" Sophie was brought to her feet and watched as they drew Winnie and Ben from their truck as well.

"They'll have to do," she overheard Reg and the other gangsters muttered to each other. "Boss'll be here any minute and this has got to go down tonight."

Suddenly, the Valentine's Day Massacre suddenly popped into Sophie's head for some reason. *What was that about again?* she struggled to remember when a creaky warehouse door edged open, entering the one called Boss. Boss was paunchier than the other gangsters, but dressed just as smart in a slate tux, spatterdashes, a fedora, and an overcoat. A fat cigar hung from his big lips. Some of "his men" flanked him; "his men" being other armed mobsters or law enforcement he paid.

Boss strolled in, stopping in front of what the cat brought in. He growled Reg's name after looking them over, clearly not pleased with the oversight either.

"The Jay Street Gang is ten blocks away!" Announced a young cronie appearing from nowhere. He must have been a spy or a lookout. "*They* have the mayor's daughter!"

"Aww, see now! Ya can't blame me!" Reg defended.

"I'd bet the farm they're trying to frame you, Boss," Another mobster said.

Boss furled his hard face at the news. He was aiming

to persuade the city mayor to amend the prohibition regulations in his favor (with his daughter as collateral). For months, he and his gang stockpiled booze and prepared businesses for the ventures that would come from the changes. The Jay Street Gang were his rivals from another city, intent on claiming his loot for their own. Perhaps the mayor's daughter was their collateral too. Company was the last thing he wanted tonight, but at least he could be prepared.

"Carlton, Stewart, with me!" Boss turned on his heels and strode back out of the warehouse. The men he called to join him were his cops. They were leaving to move forward with his visit to the mayor. "The rest of you, hold the base! They don't leave this city with a drop!"

His remaining gangsters armed themselves and talked strategies to prepare for the skirmish, seeming to care little about the hostages. The preoccupation gave Timothy an opportunity to sneak into the warehouse to help his friends. The fear in their faces switched to hope and delight when he discovered them. The getting-out part was the most nerve-racking though.

Timothy began with unbinding Sophie, working to undo the ropes as fast as he could with his pocket knife and trembling hands. On more than one occasion, he had to duck out of sight so a passing gangster wouldn't catch him. Gun fire told them the opposing gang was within shooting distance as well, making him more jittery.

By all appearances, the fight migrated into the building by the time Sophie was free. Their hearing was dulled by the gunfire, closed entrances were shot at or kicked in, gang members rushed to and fro across the lot, often confronting one other just yards away from the hostages. Timothy moved on to freeing Winnie next, though he was shaking like a leaf at that point.

What she would have given to help. She watched a couple gangsters in combat close by, hoping one of them had a knife or something on hand. One with his back to them was shot and dropped to the floor, blowing their cover. Still bloodthirsty, the gunman took aim at them. Without a second thought, Sophie cried out a warning and leaped between her friends and the oncoming bullet shower. She barely felt her body hit the concrete floor and every inch of her quaked as she tried to get upright again. Weakness and dizziness kept her to the ground.

"Where am I?" She wondered as she stared into the rafters. Blurry bodies hung over her, calling her name and trying to tend to her.

"Sophie! Sophie!"

Slowly slipping into shock, she was too tired to acknowledge any address, but she still heard her name, getting more emphatic and repetitive, as if someone were trying to wake her up. Sophie closed her eyes on the warehouse skirmish but opened them to see her dad, sitting next to her on her own bed in her own bedroom-- completely uninjured and still in her "glad rag" sleep attire-- just a few minutes after midnight 2020.

"Sophie, since you're writing your paper on the 1920's, I thought some family history could help." Sophie's dad offered her a memory book of old photos and keepsakes.

"This is your great-grandmother, Alwinda." He introduced as he opened the book. "Your mother and I gave you her name as your middle name." He singled out a portrait of her relative, looking just like the younger lady Sophie saw in her out-of-time experience. "Great-grandma Winnie!" Sophie recalled to herself. "That's why she was so familiar!" She was laid to rest while Sophie was still young, but she never forgot the scent of her perfume. A beach postcard showed that Grandma Winnie and her aunt actually vacationed in Florida.

"This assignment would be cake if I could still talk to her," Sophie thought, but the snapshots and mementos left behind from her life spoke all she needed to know. She took notes from the stories her dad told her about the photographs. None of which involved a hostage situation with the mafia, but there was still a Ben Westin whom her great-grandmother dated and later married.

Suddenly, history, once so tedious and distant to her, was interesting and physically at her fingertips! Impassioned, she moved onto making a memory board above her desk, pinning up the photos and cutouts and pairing them with ideas and highlights written on sticky notes. Satisfied with the arrangement, she stood back, looking over it with pride. She forgot it was the wee hours of the new year. Filling her mind instead was how she had a lot of exciting things to write about in her essay, and couldn't wait to take her fresh start.

"My great-grandmother, Alwinda Catherine Brady, helps bring the former century to life for me." She typed. "She was a young adult one-hundred years ago, so she was in the perfect position to experience the changing tides of society and technology."

She drew from her memory board as she continued her essay. Her great-grandmother also kept a journal and letters from her pen-pals, so Sophie easily found details to portray about daily life and events of the time. She especially liked entries about voting for the first time, traveling, dancing to jazz music, and seeing movies. Liking those things herself, Sophie imagined she'd get along well with her great-grandmother if she could know more of her in the 1920's. "Maybe I get it from her," she mused with a smile, gazing at her portrait on the board.

Sophie forgot sleep until she finished typing,

concluding her first draft at three in the morning. While her effort just to put together a well-written essay was a big step in the direction of a passing grade, she spent the rest of the week proofreading and editing for good measure. She figured she couldn't take anymore chances on her work, that every little detail she could get would count, and that she had to make her great-grandmother proud with her own hard work.

After reviewing Sophie's essay, her English teacher offered her an extra credit opportunity to present her essay, which only a few other students had done. Sophie couldn't pass up the chance. Not only for the sake of her grade, but for the pleasure of talking about all that she learned from her great-grandmother. From there, Sophie resolved to learn more about Great-grandmother Winnie's lifetime and be attentive and diligent enough to pass her English class in the process too. She finally understood why things like the stock market and the Valentine's Day Massacre were important to the decade. Beyond the first month of the year, the dress she wore in her dream-experience was still vivid in her memory by the time spring formal was scheduled. She managed to get it recreated and updated for the event. In the end, she saved her spring break freedom and even started reading more.

Sophie Westin

Mrs. Myers

10th grade English, 3rd period

January 13, 2020

1920's Essay

English historian John Dalberg-Acton said, "history is not a burden on the memory, but an illumination of the soul." Learning historical facts at first seems like a laborious task of studying the past. While facts tell us that in the 1920's, women gained the right to vote, the selling and production of alcohol was prohibited, and the first city skyscrapers were built, my great-grandmother, Alwinda Catherine Brady, either witnessed or experienced life with these facts newly in motion. She helps bring the former century to life for me. She was a young adult one-hundred years ago, so she was in the perfect position to experience the changing tides of society and technology. The legacy she left behind for my family enlightens a lot of common facts about the decade and even shines light on lesser-known ones.

Facts merely attempt to explain the social changes in women's lives during the 1920's. In addition to the right to vote, more women worked outside the home, enabling them to gain personal independence. Birth control was also first developed, and women smoking and drinking became more socially acceptable. Women's fashion drastically changed as well with rising hemlines on skirts and dresses and the increase in cosmetics. However, according to family records and stories, the social changes made growing up difficult for my great-grandmother. Born in a small town of Ferris Creek where she lived for sixteen years, many people of the community expected her at a young age to act ladylike and prepare for being a wife and mother, but my great-grandmother had little interest in the traditional family life at the time. The Ferris Creek community was reluctant to accept many of the new developments as well, to the point of thinking my great-grandmother was becoming a scandalous woman because she left the store with rouge and a radical fashion magazine one time. In reality, my great-grandmother was only curious about the new, progressive styles. She went on to live a respectable life, just in a liberal manner that clashed with Ferris Creek's antiquated ideals.

So eventually, my great-grandmother moved to the city where she lived with her aunt, who established herself there after becoming widowed after World War I. My great-grandmother was finally able to live life as she wanted. For instance, she wanted to be called Winnie for short, cut her hair into the popular bob style, and wear the makeup and shorter clothing without so much high judgement. Also, when she moved in, her aunt encouraged her to find work so she could help with living expenses and earn her own spending money. The two of them worked in a department store.

Facts will also point out many innovations in leisure activities and entertainment took shape in the 1920's. Jazz was the popular style of music, often heard in speakeasies, clubs, or even in the comfort of one's home through radio or records. Movies with sound were introduced. Even the idea of a vacation emerged as more people owned an automobile and came by the time and money to spare on long-distance trips. Infrastructure was improved and hotels were developed to accommodate travelers as well. Even before Great-grandma Winnie moved to the city, she and her own parents would spend a weekend there with her aunt to watch films, dine in a fancy restaurant, see a play or music show, or partake in other activities the city offered. Being able to do something fun nearly any night she wanted to was her favorite part of living in the city. Later on, Winnie and her aunt planned their own vacation to Florida when the state was experiencing a land boom.

I believe my grandmother just wanted to be a teenager before she moved to the city, and such an idea is one thing that typical facts may omit regarding the 1920's. Before that point, little transition came between children and adults. As soon as they were capable, young people were often sent to work or given other grown-up responsibilities in order to help provide for their families. However, compulsory school attendance regulations were established early in the decade, moving more young people from industrial labor to the classroom, and thus granting them more opportunities to be around other people their age. Advancements in home-based products simplified housework, providing them free time at home, as well. Courtesy of the automobile, they could also travel to visit one another or spend time in new and exciting places.. Even the causal sense of dating developed prominence as all the changes propelled the generation away from antiquated traditions involving marriage.

Studying history through my great-grandmother's life, I see how she came of age during a thriving, frivolous moment in American history. While the textbook facts merely describe the changes and events, my great-grandmother documented the experiences that affected her, like gaining the right to vote and the opportunity to work. Her life also casts a light on lesser-known facts like Florida's real estate boom, and the fresh ideas of adolescence, dating, and vacationing. Learning the facts of history alone may be boring at first, but they were the backdrop of my great-grandma Winnie's existence and ultimately the foundation of my own.

ABOUT KATIE JOHNS

Katharine "Katie" Johns is a college friend of James' and graduated from West Virginia State University with a bachelor's degree specializing in English Education. In her spare time, she is an English and writing tutor, an occasional blogger, and just journals and free-writes any chance she gets. She especially enjoys that classic literature through Amazon is either free or cheap!

AUNT CHARLOTTE OF SHEFFIELD

Daniel is not excited when his mother forces him to spend part of the summer with his snobby aunt in her ritzy beach community. Things quickly take a turn during their visit when Daniel discovers that his Aunt Charlotte is keeping a secret. It challenges Daniel's idea of reality and if discovered could put himself and his family in jeopardy.

AUNT CHARLOTTE OF SHEFFIELD

By Ted Garcia

AUNT CHARLOTTE OF SHEFFIELD

"I don't want to go to Aunt Charlotte's house!" I groaned as my mother packed up my suitcase. She turned to glare at me momentarily and then continued packing without saying a word. "She doesn't even like me. She's so mean. I'm convinced she's a witch."

My mother paused and took a deep breath. "Don't be so dramatic," she said. "She lives in a beautiful house right on the beach. You don't even realize how lucky you are. Do you know how many kids in your class would kill to spend time in this gorgeous house on the beach? Besides we haven't seen her for a year. We are due for another visit." I brought my head down in defeat. I had no idea how I was going to get through the next few days.

Later that day, I reluctantly dragged my feet to the car and threw my suitcase in the trunk. My dad gave me a smile. "Are you ready to hit the road?" I stayed silent and pretended not to hear him. I hopped into the back seat and put in my earbuds, staring blankly out the window. It was a gorgeous summer day, but a dark cloud loomed over my head.

The four hour drive to Sheffield Beach dragged on. Once I could see the "Welcome to Sheffield Beach" sign, a shiver went down my spine. My mom was right that a teenage boy should be excited to spend some summertime down by the shore in a big beautiful house, but I wasn't. My Aunt Charlotte was my mother's sister. Technically she was her half sister who was fifteen years older. They were not close when they were younger in part due to their large age gap, but once they got older my mom put in the effort to build their relationship. I wish she hadn't. Aunt Charlotte was a single, miserable old woman with no enjoyment in life other than being a crotchety bitch.

At one point she had been married. My Uncle Al was older than her. He was more bearable to spend time with than she was, but we weren't close. They weren't even that close with each other. Even when I was a young kid I could see that there was no love between them. It was obvious that she had married him for his money. Aunt Charlotte and my mother grew up in poverty. My mom reminisces about her childhood with fondness, while Aunt Charlotte seems to look back on it with disdain.

Uncle Al died of kidney disease a few years back. Aunt Charlotte didn't shed a single tear at his funeral. As a matter of fact the next day she went to a dealership and got herself a brand new car.

As soon as we pulled onto Rumson Drive, my stomach turned. I could see her house looming over us. It was honestly a really nice house. It was a Cape Cod covered in shingles and varying shades of grey. She kept it in good condition with a well-manicured lawn and fountain out front with a garden that was filled with fragrant flowers. In the back was a short sandy pathway that led directly to the beach. I groaned and dad put the car in park.

I could see the beach past the row of houses. The waves gently rolled onto the sand as seagulls flapped through the air in droves. The window of the car was down and I could smell the salty air. I could feel the warmth of the hot sun heating up my leg. It was such a beautiful town with such a miserable resident.

As we began unloading our things, Aunt Charlotte walked out from her home. She was a stylish woman with a short grey bob, striking green eyes, and lacked the wrinkles that most women her age had. "Sarah," she cooed. My mother ran up to her in an embrace. "Charlotte, it's been too long. You look great!"

Aunt Charlotte looked her up and down. "Well you certainly look tired. Please everyone come in. Rosemary, will you please help them with their bags." Rosemary was my Aunt Charlotte's housekeeper. I have no idea why an unemployed, single woman needs a housekeeper, but she had one.

"Of course," Rosemary ran up to my dad and took the bag from his hand. I felt bad for Rosemary. She had worked for my Aunt Charlotte for quite some time and was consistently treated badly. She also had to be near seventy and did all the work in and out of my aunt's home including landscaping and other manual labor. She lived with my aunt and I often wondered if she had a family of her own.

"Oh that's really not necessary, Rosemary." my father insisted. "We hardly have any bags. We're only staying for a few days."

"Oh Pete," Aunt Charlotte laughed. "Please, I want you to relax and enjoy yourself." My father reluctantly handed Rosemary our bags and we all followed her into the house."

"Is this all new furniture?" my mother asked.

"Yes it is. I can't bear to keep the same living room set for more than a year," Aunt Charlotte said. "It was designed by Cameron Feinstein. The one with the interior designing show on the home network. It cost an absolute fortune, but it was so worth it. He has the best taste," Aunt Charlotte grinned and sat on her couch. "Maybe for

Christmas this year I could have him redo your living room. God knows it could use it."

My mom cleared her throat. "Thank you Charlotte, but we're happy with what we have. Right Pete?"

"I mean our couch isn't bad but I won't turn down the chance to get the living room redone." My mother shot him a glare. "On second thought I don't think I could part with our living room furniture."

Aunt Charlotte's dagger eyes came to me. "And how are you, Daniel? Oh my, that acne looks much worse than I remembered. I've seen recent pictures of you online but it sure looks angrier in person. I have the best dermatologist here in Sheffield. Maybe I could set you up for an appointment while you're all here."

I recoiled in embarrassment. "Yeah, maybe."

"Is school going well for you, dear? I know you weren't doing very well last school year. There's no shame in repeating a grade," Aunt Charlotte took a sip from the wine glass on the end table next to her. "Some people really need it."

"Actually, Daniel is doing great in school this year," my mother interjected. "He had straight A's and joined the track team, which he is doing amazing in. Aren't you, honey?"

"Yeah I like it." I said curtly.

Aunt Charlotte twirled her wine glass in her hand.

"Well, I'm glad to hear you've turned things around." She brought her icy stare back to my parents and continued on with a mundane conversation about her beautiful house, rich friends, blah blah blah. I have never met someone that liked to brag as much as her.

That night I laid in my bed in a huff. *I can't believe I have to be here,* I thought. *Why does mom even want to come here to see her sister? She isn't nice to any of us. Being family isn't a reason to put up with someone that treats you like garbage.* I sighed and turned over onto my side in bed. I got my own room when we visited Aunt Charlotte since she lived in such a large house. That was the only good thing about coming to visit. Having my own room meant I had an escape.

I glanced at the clock which read: 1:17. I couldn't sleep. My mind was racing and I still had a lot of frustration built up from wasting a day spending time with the witch of Sheffield Beach. I stood up and walked over to the window, gazing out at the ocean. It was peaceful seeing the light ripples of the water. The moon reflected on the waves. I opened the window slightly and could feel a light breeze blow in. I closed my eyes for a minute and pretended that I was somewhere else. *It's only a week,* I told myself.

Once I opened my eyes again I could see a figure moving out onto the dock. I squinted my eyes to try to get a clearer look. It was a slender figure that appeared to be a woman. It looked like my Aunt Charlotte. *Why is she up so late?* The figure walked to the end of the dock and bent over the side. I could see the figure cranking something which appeared to be lifting up a rope. The rope held a large net which I could see something flopping around in. It was some kind of huge fish. I could see its tail writhing. The figure unhooked the net and swung it onto the dock before turning around pulling it with them.

I ducked down, fearing that if it was Aunt Charlotte she'd see me staring out at her. *What was that huge fish? Why was Aunt Charlotte trying to catch a fish at one in the morning anyway?* I peered back out the window, but there was no one in sight. Suddenly I could hear a door close downstairs. *It was Aunt Charlotte outside!*

I opened the door and listened carefully. I couldn't hear anything. I tiptoed out of my room and over to the stairs. I peeked down to see if I could see her, but I couldn't. I could, however, hear the sound of footsteps. I considered whether or not to go down the stairs to investigate what was going on. My curiosity got the best of me and I slowly made my way down the stairs, doing my best not to make any noise. The house was completely dark only being slightly lit by the street lamps outside. The stairs slightly creaked underneath me. For such a new house it sure did make a lot of noise.

I peered around the corner to see if I could see my aunt. She was nowhere in sight, but I could hear another door shut quietly. It had to be the basement. I made my way over to the basement door and pressed my ear up against it. I could hear a thumping on the stairs. It had to be the fish getting dragged down the stairs. Suddenly the noise stopped. I took a deep breath, scared to open it up and see what was on the other side. I reached out my sweaty palm to gently turn the knob. I could clearly hear more flopping and my Aunt Charlotte grumbling something, although I couldn't make out exactly what it was that she was saying. I gently shut the door again and scurried into the dining room planning on waiting until Aunt Charlotte went to bed to investigate what was going on down in the basement.

I crawled underneath the kitchen table to wait it out. After some time I could see the basement door slowly open and my aunt's feet gingerly move across the living room floor and up the stairs, out of sight. I waited for a little while to make sure that she was staying up there. Afterwards, I slipped out from under the table and made my way over to the basement door. I looked both ways to make sure that no one was coming and opened the door.

I stared down into the darkness. I could feel my legs shaking. I had no idea what I was going to find down there. I slowly began to make my way down the creaky stairs. I had never gone down into the basement before. I began feeling around the walls for a light switch until I felt a string slide across my face. I pulled on it and the dim light from the bulb lit the room.

Once my eyes adjusted to the light I was able to see the room quite clearly. There was a wet, metal table with wheels. Cardboard boxes and bubble wrap lined the walls. Above the boxes were what appeared to be plaques. I moved closer and could see that the plaques had fish fins on them. Each plaque had a small gold engraving that said "Sheffield Beach, RI" with different dates. I turned around and saw a massive tank. I stopped short and my body began to tremble. I could see something swimming in the murky water of the tank. I took in a deep breath and moved closer to the tank.

I could see the water swirling with the movements of the fish inside of it. *What is this? A shark?* It was a colossal tank that must have just as big of an animal living inside of it. The net that Aunt Charlotte pulled up on the dock appeared to be huge. Suddenly I saw something press against the glass. *Is that...? No. It can't be!* A human hand was pressed up against the glass.

I fell to the ground in shock. That was a human hand. There was no question in my mind. There isn't a fish in this tank. It's a person! I turned around and ran up the stairs as fast as my feet would carry me.

Once back in my bedroom I jumped into the bed, still shaking. I had so many questions running through my mind. *Why did Aunt Charlotte trap a person in a net? Why is she keeping them in a tank? I thought I saw a fish tail flopping around on the deck; was that just a figment of my imagination?* I breathed heavily and put my head in my hands, feeling an overwhelming sensation of nausea. *I need to tell my parents about this. I don't think we're safe here.*

My eyes opened the next morning and I immediately began to question whether what I had seen last night was all a dream. There is no way that could have been real. Aunt Charlotte was a nasty person, but she wouldn't have some kind of weird torture chamber in her basement. I got up and stretched looking out my window at the dock. *That was a dream, wasn't it?*

"Daniel," my mother called from down the stairs. "Come get your breakfast." I walked down the stairs and the smell of bacon and eggs entered my nostrils immediately. I normally love the smell of a fresh-cooked breakfast, but today it filled me with dread. How was I supposed to act like everything was normal after what I saw last night? I sat down at the dining room table, which I had just hidden under hours before.

Rosemary laid a plate of food in front of me and I just stared at it. I looked down at the bacon that was still sizzling, the fluffy, yellow scrambled eggs, and the golden pancakes laid on top of one another. My stomach churned.

"Not hungry?" my dad asked. "Normally you'd inhale that without even chewing. Are you feeling okay?"

"Yes, I'm fine. I'm just not very hungry right now." I turned my head down to face the table.

"Well you did have a late night last night, didn't you?" my Aunt Charlotte, questioned with a smirk.

"What do you mean?" my mother asked.

"Well I could hear Daniel running around the house last night. It was very late. I'm not sure what he was doing. Perhaps playing tag with an imaginary friend," Aunt Charlotte took a sip of coffee.

Do I call her out right here and now? "I was just up a lot going to the bathroom," I said with a shrug. I couldn't say anything right in front of her. I needed to be a little more sneaky.

"Ah," Aunt Charlotte said. "Well then you should lay off the soda. It makes you pee all the time and I'm sure it doesn't help with that acne."

My mother shifted uncomfortably in her chair. "I'd love to go lay out on the beach today." my mom said, changing the subject.

"It is quite a beautiful private beach that we have here in this community," Aunt Charlotte said. "I may come out and join you, but I have a bit of work to do first." I looked up at her and her gaze met mine. "Would you like to help me, Daniel?"

I froze and began to stammer. "I... uh... sure. If you need me to."

After breakfast, my parents headed out to the beach expecting me to join them after helping my Aunt Charlotte with what she needed. Once the front door shut behind them Aunt Charlotte turned to me. "You were down in the basement." Her face was emotionless and cold.

"I just heard something downstairs. I was seeing what it was. I'm sorry. I just.."

"Enough," she interrupted. "What did you see?"

I didn't know how honest to be. I figured she probably already knew what I knew and decided to tell the whole truth. "I saw some boxes and a tank and some plaques on the wall."

She smirked. "You saw my mermaid."

"Your what?" I asked.

"My mermaid." She moved over to the couch and sat down. "Please, sit."

My entire body was trembling, but I followed her and sat down.

"You're quite a nosey boy. I bet you've never seen something so magnificent before," Aunt Charlotte turned her body. "Rosemary, dear, could you please bring us some cookies." Rosemary nodded from the edge of the kitchen.

"What do you mean a mermaid?" I tried my best to keep my voice steady and look relaxed.

"I mean a mermaid. Not quite like what you may see in the movies. In reality they aren't quite as pretty, but they are very real. Their existence isn't very well known, but there is a market for them and those that do know about them will pay a pretty penny for their fins." Rosemary set the cookies down on the coffee table in front of us. "I was hoping to keep this as hush hush as possible, but now you know. Your parents can know nothing about this."

I thought back to seeing the large fin flopping on the dock and seeing the hand pressed against the glass of the tank. It made sense now, but how was this possible? "You sell their fins?"

"I do. Normally Rosemary helps me to catch them and brings them down into my workshop, but the poor thing's back has been bothering her. Isn't that right, Rosemary?"

Rosemary nodded, avoiding eye contact as she placed a pitcher of water next to the platter of cookies.

"You know that your parents can't know about this. There is a very elite, select few that are even aware of the existence of these creatures and we can't have any chance of it becoming public knowledge."

I stammered, completely bewildered by what I was hearing. "How did you find out that they existed?"

Aunt Charlotte adjusted herself in the chair. "My husband was a finsman before his death."

"A finsman?" I asked.

"Yes. When he would catch these creatures, we would cut off their fins, mount them, and sell them for profit." Aunt Charlotte casually took a bite of a cookie, despite the gruesome description. "Now I continue his work. We have to pay our bills somehow."

"So... you kill them?" I asked, gulping hard.

"No I don't kill them," Aunt Charlotte said, letting out a little laugh as if I'd told a joke. "We cut off their fins and release them back into the ocean."

"But they wouldn't be able to swim, would they?" I asked.

"You sure have a lot of questions, Daniel. To be frank, I don't know what happens when we dump them into the ocean and I don't particularly care." Her eyes narrowed on me. "Let me be totally transparent with you. This is what I do for work. Just like how your mom and dad go to work to pay the bills for your home. This is what I do to pay the bills for mine. I don't want anything bad to happen to you, my sister, or your father, but if this gets out I will have no choice. Do we understand each other?"

I gulped. "Yes," I said, barely audible.

Aunt Charlotte's expression lightened. "Good. Well why don't you put on your swimsuit and join your parents out at the beach. It's a gorgeous day." I hardly had a chance to respond before she stood up and left me alone in the living room. My mind was going all over the place. If she had not just sat me down and bluntly confirmed what I had seen was true I may have convinced myself that it was all a dream. I had to face the reality that this was fact and not fiction. I felt like I had to warm my parents. My aunt was a horrible person, but I had never seen her get violent before. Still I knew that what she was saying to me was a threat to myself and my family. I had to warn them to get us out of here as soon as possible.

I quickly got dressed in a daze and headed out toward the beach. My mind was racing as I walked toward my parents. *Do I tell them about what's going on? Will they even believe me? What will Aunt Charlotte do if she finds out that I told them?* I could hardly even believe that this was happening, there was no way I could expect my parents to believe any of this especially considering the fact that they knew I hated Aunt Charlotte's guts. They may think that I'd be willing to make up any kind of outlandish story as an excuse to go back home.

I approached my parents who were both casually relaxing in red beach chairs, completely oblivious to what was going in in Aunt Charlotte's house. "Hi, honey," my mom turned to greet me. "Isn't it gorgeous out here today?" My parents were both covered in sunscreen and in their swimsuits. They looked so relaxed. I so wished I could have been as blissfully unaware as they were.

I nodded, trying my best to look normal.

"What's wrong?" she asked, crinkling her brows. *How do mothers always know when something's wrong?*

"Nothing," I said with a plastered fake smile. "I was just helping Aunt Charlotte clean up a bit.

"Why was Aunt Charlotte cleaning? Isn't Rosemary working today?"

Darn it!

"Uh... yeah she is, but there was a lot to clean up I guess so she was wondering if I could help too."

My mother put her hands on her hips. "He's lying to me, Pete."

Dad turned over on his reclined beach chair. "Tell your mother the truth, Daniel." He sounded half asleep.

I sighed in exasperation. "It's nothing. Aunt Charlotte was mad at me because I was going around the house late last night when I should have been sleeping. Okay? Now can I please swim?"

"Why would Aunt Charlotte care if you were walking around the house? She doesn't have anything to hide."

"Oh yes she does," I immediately covered my mouth. *Crap.* I had blurted it out before I had a chance to even think about what I was saying. There was no going back now. I had to tell my mom the whole truth.

"What do you mean?" my mother's expression turned from confused to concerned.

"I heard her come into the house late last night. I went down there to see what she was up to and saw her go into the basement. Once she came back up I went down there and saw this huge tank with what I thought was a fish in it." I took a deep breath. "It turns out it's a mermaid. Aunt Charlotte is a psycho that cuts off their fins and sells them. That's why she's so rich."

"Oh my God." My mother stood there, mouth agape. "You are on drugs. Daniel what did you take? This isn't funny. I need you to tell me this instant. Pete, we're taking him to the hospital." My dad sighed and stood up, used to my mother's frequent overreactions.

"Stop! I'm serious. I'm not on any kind of drugs. I know it doesn't sound real, but that's why Aunt Charlotte asked me to stay back with her. She didn't need my help with anything. She was threatening me saying that I better not tell anybody about what I know. Please, you can't tell her."

"Daniel," my mother said quietly. "I know that Aunt Charlotte is a little eccentric, but there is no such thing as mermaids. You and I both know that.

"Then how did she make all of her money?"

Mom thought for a moment. "Your Uncle Ron was a businessman. He was very successful."

"And did he ever say what kind of business he was in?"

"Well it was... I think it was..." my mother continued to think. "What did he do, Pete?"

My dad shrugged.

"If you don't believe me then wait until tonight. I'll show you myself, but don't mention anything to Aunt Charlotte."

My mother turned to my father, both silent. I couldn't blame them. I'd have no idea what to say in this situation either. Then they turned back to me and silently nodded.

That night I laid awake in bed continually looking over at the clock. I figured that once 2 am hit, Aunt Charlotte would be in bed for sure. I kept checking out the window at the dock to look for her. I didn't know how often she caught these creatures and I wanted to make sure that the coast was clear. I didn't see her out there. Once two am hit, I crept out to my parent's bedroom. My dad was loudly snoring and I could see the whites of my mother's eyes in the dark room. She was lying awake waiting for me.

"Dad wake up," I said, shaking him. "It's time."

I led them down the creaky stairs to the basement door. For a moment I questioned my own sanity. *What if that was just all a dream? I'm going to look like a total nutcase.* I held firm in what I saw though and opened the door. "Be careful," I whispered. "The light is at the bottom of the stairs."

Once we reached the bottom I pulled the now familiar light's string. My parents were facing me. My parent's eyes were locked on the plaques that hung across the top of the wall. My mom's mouth was agape. She walked closer to them. "How is this possible? This isn't possible." She gently brushed her hand over the fins. She looked closer at one of the engravings and read it carefully.

"Look behind you," I said. They both turned around and I could see their eyes widen. The tank towered in front of us. I could see the water swirling with the mermaid circling inside the tank. I stepped closer and could see glimpses of the creature in the water. The water was pretty dirty and opaque. You could only see it as it got close to the glass facing us. I couldn't make out exactly what it looked like. I knew it had human hands which I had seen last night and I knew that it had a fishtail which I had seen flopping around on the deck when Aunt Charlotte pulled it out of the water. I wondered if there were others in the tank with it.

"Damn," my dad said in a hushed tone.

My mother put her hands over her mouth as if that was the only thing that was preventing her from screaming. "It's true." Her voice squeaked. "What the hell is that?"

"I told you guys. It's a mermaid. They exist, but most people don't know about it. Aunt Charlotte doesn't want people to know about it. Apparently the fins sell for a ton of money." My eyes were locked on the tank. Suddenly hands pressed against the glass for a moment and then disappeared into the gray water.

My mother slowly dropped to the floor and sat down when she saw the hands. "Oh my God this can't be real." She put her hands on top of her head. "What do we do? Do we call the police? This is sick. Those were human hands!" She closed her eyes. I could see her rocking on the floor. It looked almost as if she was having a panic attack.

"What could the police do?" my dad said. "This isn't technically a crime, because there aren't laws written about mermaids." He paused for a moment. "I can't believe those words just came out of my mouth." He knelt down and rubbed my mother's back. "It's okay. There has to be some reasonable explanation for this. The ocean is so expansive there are parts of it that have never been explored. This must just be a type of fish that hasn't been discovered yet."

My mother shot up and walked to the basement stairs. "Well we aren't staying here. Pack your bags. We're leaving tonight."

"But we can't just leave it here. She's going to cut off it's fins and dump it back into the ocean. It's going to die. That's inhumane. We can't let that happen." I said.

"Well we are not staying here another minute," my mom said, firmly. "We will call the police from the car. They can decide what to do from there"

"I don't think so," a voice said from the top of the stairs. It was Aunt Charlotte. She slowly made her way down the stairs. "Calling the police on your own sister? I knew you didn't have money, but you obviously lack class as well." She stood in front of us dressed in an apron and rubber boots. Her face looked emotionless. She didn't look angry or surprised, just blank. It was scarier seeing her have no expression than seeing her have an angry outburst.

"This is sick, Charlotte. We're going home. I don't want my family to have any part of this" my mom said.

"I didn't plan to have you be a part of it. I don't plan to start now either." Aunt Charlotte pulled a gun out from under her coat. She aimed it directly at my mother.

"Charlotte, what are you doing?" my mother said, voice trembling.

"I don't want to hurt my family, but you've really left me no choice." Suddenly I heard a click up the stairs. It was the door shutting and locking from the outside. I heard more footsteps coming down the stairs. It was Rosemary. "You came just in time for the show," Aunt Charlotte said, wild-eyed. She moved the gun from my mother to my father and finally to me.

Rosemary made her way over to the tank and dangled raw meat into the water. Suddenly the creature shot up from the water and hooked onto the meat. Rosemary grabbed it by its long hair. It had a long scaly tail and what appeared to be a man's torso, but it was completely green. It had sharp teeth that I could see biting into the meat and several black eyes, almost looking like the eyes of a fly.

"Oh you didn't expect these beasts to be gentle, did you?" my aunt said, looking directly at me. "You know that they are one of the biggest predators in the sea. They will eat anything, living or dead. You don't want to be swimming in the same water as them." She aimed the gun at each of us.

Rosemary dragged the creature over to the table surrounded by boxes. She was an old woman, but she was showing a crazy amount of strength. She was quite large and I never considered the fact that could have been solid muscle. It wiggled and its tail slapped the metal table making a loud bang. She strapped it to the table using belts that were attached and then went underneath and pulled out a saw. *Oh no*, I thought. *She's going to cut off the fins.*

"Wait!" I yelled. "Aunt Charlotte, I want to help."

Aunt Charlotte gave me an icy, unwavering glare. "Help me?"

"I think this whole thing is pretty cool. Teach me how to do it. I want to help you. These things are pretty big. I could help catch them and carry them down here. We could do it as a team." I tried my best to look relaxed and keep a steady breath.

"You want to help me?" Aunt Charlotte squinted.

"Yes. Show me how to do this." I walked toward Rosemary and the creature which continued to squirm. As I approached it I could see mucus covered gills moving in and out in a failed attempt to breathe.

Aunt Charlotte walked toward me. "I don't think that I can trust you. Besides, if you're as bad at this as you are at school, you'd be no help to me anyway." She had finally lowered the gun. Now was the time.

As soon as she got close to me I shoved her as hard as I could. Just as I had hoped, she lost her grip on the gun and it dropped to the ground. I slid it to my parents. "Grab it!" I yelled. Both of my parents dove for the gun.

My mother got there first and lifted it, aiming at her sister.

"Stay back, Charlotte," she said. She turned to my dad. "Call the police," she commanded. My dad ran up the basement stairs.

I breathed heavily and kept a watchful eye on Rosemary and Aunt Charlotte. Rosemary had dropped the saw and stood back. Aunt Charlotte had her dagger eyes locked on my mother. "You would do this to your own sister?" she said. "I could share the money if that's what you want. We could split it fifty-fifty."

"Some things are worth more than money." she looked over at me and smiled slightly.

I could hear the police come through the front door moments later. Three cops came down the basement stairs followed by my father. They stopped short when they saw the creature on the table. After a momentary pause, they cuffed Rosemary and my aunt and took them away.

"We'll have animal control take care of that." one of the police said, motioning toward the creature.

"No," I said. "I know what to do." I walked over to one side of the table and grabbed on. "Dad, help me." He walked over to me and together we lifted the table and carried it up the stairs. We walked across the sand to the dock. Once we reached the end of the dock we tilted the table and my mother carefully undid the straps. The creature slid into the water. I waited for a moment to see if it would resurface, but it didn't.

"I'm proud of you." my mom said and smiled at me. "I'm sorry for not believing you. You saw Aunt Charlotte for what she really was."

I looked out onto the water thinking about what other things lurk in the deep, dark sea. It gave me a slight chill. Once this police report was out in the public the world would know that mermaids exist. Although they are not the beautiful, gentle creatures that are talked about in fairy tales. It would be a while before I ever felt comfortable enough to swim in the ocean. I didn't want to see this thing get butchered, but I also don't want to swim with it. "Just please promise me one thing, mom."

She walked up to me and put her arm on my shoulder. "What?"

I turned to her and smirked, "You let me pick where we go on vacation next summer."

ABOUT TED GARCIA

Ted Garcia is a teacher residing in New Jersey who enjoys writing short stories in various genres. When he isn't writing or teaching he enjoys spending time outdoors, traveling, and participating in community theater.

THE HEART HEALER

To everyone else, Lily was just a normal fifteen-year-old girl whose parents were genius scientists. Unbeknownst to others, Lily was a cardiac patient who suffered from anxiety and was going to require surgery to live. As her condition worsened, she struggled through isolation as others began to see her non-normal side and avoided her. Lily was alone and scared until one fateful day she came across a dog that changed everything. Join Lily in her journey to freedom as she undergoes a strange adventure that ends up changing the lives of millions.

THE HEART HEALER

By Lorraine Bradner

ONE

THE DAY EVERYTHING CHANGED

I sat on the steps of my school and watched as the other students laughed with each other, swapped handshakes, and all got on the bus or went to their cars. By this point, even though I'm only fifteen, being an outsider is something I'm used to. I can't blame them though; It's hard to understand what I go through every day.

I suppose I'll start from the beginning. Hi. My name's Lilly, and I'm fifteen years old. My hair is a light brown color and my skin is pale. I love to wear athletic clothes and jeans with sweatshirts (which is unusual around here). I live in a small suburb in Theo, Ohio where the weather is always sunny and seventy-five with very few rainy days. Theo is a unique suburb because we have many different kinds of foliage, trees, and rules that aren't typical to most neighborhoods around here. If you walk down the streets, you'll notice a quaint symmetry among the houses. There are only two differences that you can find when looking at them. One difference is that each house alternates in color. As you look at them, you'll notice they range in color from dull green to pale blue to yellow to a pale brown. This color scheme repeats down the road on each side. The second difference you can notice in the houses is the size. Some houses are one story, while others go up to four stories. I was lucky because my parents were able to afford one of the only four-story houses on this block. If you bought a four-story house, you were lucky, because you were able to have a flat roof that you could sit on and overlook the whole town on one side. The other side, all you could see were trees from the forest. This is because even though we had a four-story house, the redwoods and willow trees were up to fifty feet tall and covered all the air space. Each house has the same tall willow tree planted on the right side in the front yard. Each house has a front yard that consists of one acre and has concrete driveways. All the backyards are one point three acres. Each backyard has a dark brown wooden fence that is two stories tall and was built with the houses when this town was created. Behind the wooden fence on my side of the street was a twenty-acre forest area filled with redwood, ash, and willow trees. When the developers conceived this town, somehow they were able to plant this forest of trees and keep them alive. I only say that because normally redwoods and willow trees can't survive next to each other because the willow trees and redwoods need so much water by themselves. They used science to make this work. My mom was a part of the project, but all I know about it is that she helped create these trees so they could live here like that.

My favorite days used to be when I could sit on the roof and see the sun poke through the tree-lines. I used to invite my friends, but now I just enjoy being alone. I think it's just better this way. It's easier to be alone. There are five other kids from my school who live on this block with me. Brett is my age and can easily be described as tall, dark, and handsome. He gets all the girls in my class. Chloe, who's fourteen, is his girlfriend. She's this beautiful African American girl with short black hair. She's always dressed in the latest trends but is still one of the most athletic girls in the school. Jess, (surprisingly, not short for Jessica), is my age and is a pale redhead with more freckles than you could imagine. Chuck, who is ten years old, is Brett's little brother. He's super short with black hair and tan skin. The last girl that lives on my block is Lola. She's my age as well and is one of the braver kids in our school. She has blonde hair in a pixie style hair cut and is always trying to con kids into doing things they shouldn't for some type of game she's made up. I met them all on the street when we first moved to this development a two years ago. I started school as a new kid since I left my old life back home in California. At first, when I moved here, we all got along. We used to play kickball on the street, run in the forest, and have game nights at my house; but that all changed after the night they saw the real me.

See, my heart doesn't work well. Yes, the one beating that is in your chest. When I was 10, I was running around and playing on the trampoline in our backyard when my heart suddenly started beating faster than it ever had before. I started breathing fast and crying. My ears started buzzing so loud that I couldn't hear much. My dad ran out to me to see what was wrong. It sounded like he was talking to me through a tunnel. Then my vision got blurry and the edges of my vision went black. The next thing I felt was my dad scooping me up. When I awoke, I was in the hospital and mom and dad were talking to some doctor. They said I had atrial fibrillation which means my heart can go up to one hundred and seventy beats per minute randomly. This happens because the upper chambers of my heart don't talk to each other properly and this causes my heart to beat weirdly. They said there was no cure and that if it gets worse as I get older, I will have to have open heart surgery.

Even though I was diagnosed when I was ten, I could still act like a normal kid most days. Sometimes though, I have an episode where it beats out of my control and causes me to pass out. Then when I wake up, it sends me into a panic attack, causing me to hyperventilate until I almost pass out again. For four years, it only would happen a few times a month. I normally would only pass out when I was really tired, but this day, the day that changed everything, was just a bad day, I guess. It was about a year ago now. Lola, of course, had made up a new game that we were playing in the forest. It was a silly game, but we were running out of games to play. In this game, whoever was named the Krumpet (Lola) had to collect small rocks and sticks. The trader (Brett) was the one who was able to talk with the Krumpet and make a deal for them. If the Krumpet didn't like the deal, then she'd be able to chase the runners (that's me, Chloe, Chuck, and Jess) and throw the rocks and sticks at us until she ran out of what was in her hand. Well, Lola had collected all her rocks and sticks and called the trader to her. For her twelve rocks and two sticks, he offered her two of his shoes. Brett's shoes are smelly, so I don't blame her for not taking the deal. She said no and yelled, "run"! I was feeling tired that day, but not too exhausted. I was laughing with Jess until Lola spotted us. We started running in between the redwoods and willow trees. This particular part of the forest only has these two trees. This is when it happened. The last thing I remember is looking over my shoulder and seeing Lola throw a long stick at me. I leaped left to grab a branch of the willow tree and then the next thing I know, I'm looking up and seeing all of them standing over me. Then my panic attack hits. All of a sudden it felt like a vacuum cleaner was sucking all the air out of me. My chest got so heavy, it didn't even feel like I had enough strength to try to breathe in the air. My legs and arms began to tingle. Next, the hyperventilating kicked in. I tried to purse my lips so I could try to breathe better, but it didn't work. Before I could stop them, my cheeks were wet with tears. *This is the worst part. Why does my body do this?*, I thought. I closed my eyes to try and focus on my breathing and grounding. I straightened out my legs and put my hands on the ground. I dug both palms into the dirt. It had rained a few days before so the soil was still moist. I felt a stick in my right hand. I tried to focus on it. That must've been the one that Lola had thrown at me. Finally, I started to feel some relief in my chest. My breathing was starting to slow down. Tears were still streaming down my face, but now it was from relief and not fear. Now a new emotion came to the surface... embarrassment. Thoughts started racing through my head as I sat on the ground still holding the stick. *What are my friends going to think? I wish they never saw this side of me. I never told them anything was ever wrong with me. They've never seen this at school because I would always be calm during recess and was always sitting during class.* For all they knew, my heart was fine. If I was having a bad heart day, mom and dad would just let me stay home.

See, my mom and dad weren't around much. My mom is a genetic developer, which meant she developed genes that would make something new and modified. For example, our town hired her to genetically change the trees so that they could all survive here. She made the redwoods get up to twenty feet tall and fifteen feet wide, the willow trees to be ten feet tall and five feet wide with full blossoming branches that created even more of a waterfall effect, and pine trees that were able to survive planted in between the redwoods and willow trees. If you didn't know, redwoods and willow trees are known to kill other trees beside them by sucking up all the water for themselves. So, it's amazing my mom was able to design these trees so they could be pretty, alive, and all survive here. Anyways, work takes up a lot of her time. She used to work at a genetic laboratory in San Diego, California, but when she took this job, we moved here. So now, she is just working at a new genetic laboratory that is actually a part of the development we live in.

My dad is also a scientist and works at the same laboratory as my mom. They work in TMO- Trees that are Modified Organisms. Dad is in charge of the laboratory and the finances they do. He basically gets the laboratory work and makes sure my mom is always kept busy. Since they are on the same schedule and doing research like this, I normally am home alone. Therefore, when I have bad days, they trust me to trust my instincts and body to get through it. If I need a note from school, they just scan one over to the school that day instead of coming home to check on me.

Most people are surprised when I tell them my parents are scientists because they don't look like it at all. My mom's name is Tracy and my dad's name is Bill. Mom looks similar to me. She has an athletic build, and is five-five with short brunette hair. (She used to weight lift and play basketball before she got consumed by her work). Dad's six-two and bald with a long gray/brown beard and is built like a lumberjack. They met during a weightlifting meet when they were younger and found out they went to the same colleges (Harvider Alumni).

Anyways, back to me. My friends were really nice to me on the walk back to the house after my episode in the forest. Chloe and Lola walked beside me and tried to rub my back and kept asking me if I was ok. They didn't ask what happened and they didn't pry to find out more. I was grateful at the time. I thought they would stick by my side unlike kids in my past. As predicted though, they all left me eventually. Once I got home, I talked to my parents and told them what had happened. Since this wasn't a usual circumstance and my fainting and panic attack occurred without a trigger, they let me stay at home the next day from school. Two days after my episode, I was back in school. I was a little embarrassed after coming back and walking into school. Our school is pretty big and has large glass windows all along the front. It opens right into a large cafeteria where kindergarten through twelfth grade sit. Branching off the cafeteria were various hallways leading off into classrooms. The first hallway on the left when you walked in was for the first graders, the second hallway was for the second graders, and so on until you were looking almost all the way to the right hallway where the twelfth graders sat. The gym and administrative offices are in a separate building that is connected through the twelfth-grade hallway. The gym has four volleyball courts, two basketball courts, and large lap pool. Then behind the gym are the softball, soccer, and football fields. In between the school and the gym is the playground where we all have recess. It's a large school, but I guess it used to be smaller. When Theo built this TMO community, they decided to renovate the school as well and created what we go to now.

There I go, going off topic again. Anyways, so there I

was walking through the clear double glass doors on this sunny day. Embarrassed about what happened and dreading seeing my friends. To make me feel better, I wore my favorite all red plain sweatshirt and black leggings so I was comfortable. As I opened the door, I turned back to face mom and waved goodbye as I watched her drive off in her new red Subaru. I closed my eyes and took a deep breath before returning to open the second set of glass doors as I prepared to see people in the cafeteria. Mom and dad had to work this morning so I was dropped off at twelve pm which is the time that grades seven through twelve are being released for lunch and recess. Mom already faxed in my note that I was sick the day before and going to be tardy today so I was allowed to go straight to lunch. I bravely lifted my head and looked to my right, towards the ninth graders table. I sighed a breath of relief when I didn't see my friends at first. I put my backpack down in a cubby by the door and headed to the lunch line to grab some food. Then I noticed them ahead of me in the lunch line. After a few minutes went by they still hadn't noticed I was behind them. I then caught a glimpse of Chloe as she turned around to look at some-thing. We made eye contact and my heart leapt. She looked like she had a hint of a smile! Then, it was weird. Lola noticed her looking at me, quickly grabbed Chloe's arm and turned her back around to face the front of the line. Lola looked at me for a second and then looked away right after that. She didn't have a smile on her face. In fact, it looked like she had just seen a monster. Lola went and whispered something to Brett and Jess. They replied in hushed tones, but didn't turn back to look at me. I started feeling anxious while I finished going through the lunch line. I didn't feel very hungry so I just grabbed a bowl of tomato soup and oyster crackers. After I got to the end of the line and paid, I turned to go towards our usual table. I noticed they didn't go to sit there. We normally sat at a round table behind the eighth graders. Instead, they were sitting at the packed long table by the other ninth and tenth graders. There was no more room for me to sit there. My palms felt sweaty under the tray. It felt like I was going to drop it. I went to our usual table and sat there alone instead of trying to find room at their table. I had a feeling they didn't want me around.

The rest of the day dragged along. I kept my head low as I walked to each class until it was time to go home. The story of what happened to me spread around the entire school. Everyone who didn't know me was staring at me, and everyone who did know me turned away. Since mom dropped me off, dad picked me up instead. I waited until everyone mostly cleared out of the hallway and cafeteria before I left through the double doors. I just didn't want to deal with people anymore. As I walked out, dad was sitting in his emerald green four door truck by the parent pick up spots. I got in the truck silently and put my backpack on the floor without looking at him. I stared out the window as we started to pull out of the parking lot. The school looks so different now. Instead of a warm inviting place, it looks like a cold desolate fearful building. Dad patted me on the head and said, "you ok, kiddo?"

"Yeah, I'm ok", I said. He looked at me again with concern and asked if i was feeling alright. I nodded my head while faking a small smile. That seemed to satisfy him. He patted me on the back and said good while we continued head on home.

TWO
THE NEW GATE

Since that day, it's been a full year. I wouldn't call them friends anymore, but the kids that I used to be friends with don't even look at my house when they walk by. My heart condition has gotten so bad that my episodes occur almost daily. The cardiologist met with me and my parents last week and said that if I didn't get the surgery soon, I was going to die. It was about five months ago when my episodes tripled and my parents took me out to school to homeschool me. I actually like it better this way. Now I don't have to deal with people staring at me and wondering if I'm going drop dead or avoiding me because they are scared of me. Some people think I'm faking it. Others just don't know how to act because they've never seen or dealt with anyone that has medical issues before.

Since my parents are never home long enough to teach me, I follow this homeschooling program that is offered online for medical patients who are unable to attend in person school instead. Because its always nice out, I am always attending "school" on my laptop while sitting on my roof. Our roof is a flat tan color that has several drainage systems on each side so that when it does rain, the water drains off the roof into underground tubs and then into the forest. This keeps the yards from flooding. We have mini redwoods, that my mother created, that sit in pots and alternate with tiki torches to help keep the bugs away. The potted redwoods and tiki torches are only at the front of the roof facing the street and on the two sides of the house that face other houses. The back view is left open so we have a clear view of the forest. Since I've started being homeschooled here, my parents set me up a desk with an outlet on the floor of the roof that's covered so I can plug in my laptop. Sitting in the sun doing schoolwork helps me with my fear and makes me feel happy. Plus, you can't beat the smell of fresh air and the view of the trees from this high up.

Sometimes I wish they didn't leave me all alone when dealing with my episodes, but I was told to be brave, so... I try to deal with it on my own. When I have episodes during the day, I have a button I can press and this calls my older neighbor over who used to be a paramedic. He has a key to the house and makes sure that I'm ok. This helps me feel a little safer. So far, he's never let me down. For a seventy-year-old man named Juan, he sure does move fast. Plus, he always brings me popsicles, which are my favorite snack. When my episode starts, I normally have five minutes before I pass out, which gives me plenty time to press the button and sit down on the cushioned couch designated for my episodes. That way I don't fall and hit my head on a hard surface. Juan normally gets here when I'm just starting to hyperventilate so it really helps me feel more comfortable with what I'm going through.

I normally go to school from eight in the morning to three in the afternoon. My parents usually get home around six or seven, so I get a few hours to play before I have to help mom with dinner. Since I play by myself, my favorite thing to do is go in my backyard and garden or draw on the fence. My mom bought me paint that washes off, so I can paint on the fence and then just wash it off when I'm done. The paint is washable for up to two days, so if I like what I painted, I leave it up for mom and dad to see before its cleaned up. I used to play basketball down the street or go running before they got home, but now the risk is too high so I have to do activities that keep my heart rate low.

Today I decided I was going to paint an elephant in a

flower field on my fence. I closed my school laptop and went down the stairs barefoot into the kitchen to grab a cold glass of water from the fridge. Then, I grabbed a protein bar from the cupboard and set them outside on the red wooden picnic table. We had a patio out back where we kept lawn furniture and a picnic table for outdoor parties. Mom and dad like to have their work friends over whenever they have a big accomplishment at work, so pretty much like every few weeks they are throwing a party. There is always something new they've developed that they want to celebrate.

Once I put my food and drink down on the picnic table, I went over to our garden shed. It's newer like our house, so it's pretty nice inside. It has pale green metal siding on it, with a tan roof and a concrete floor on the inside with shelves lining both walls. The left side and back of the shed were all for the gardening tools and dad's tools for house maintenance. The back right side of the shed is where all my paint supplies were kept. The shed was temperature controlled at 65 degrees, so my paint was never ruined. I grabbed the grey, purple, green and black buckets of paint along with a few paintbrushes and headed to the back of the fence. Every time I painted, I would choose a different part of the fence. Doing this made me feel more spontaneous and fun. Today, I thought it would be nice to paint the center of the back fence, that way when mom and dad got home and looked through the kitchen, it'd be the first thing they'd see. I set my paint buckets down and paint brushes on top of them. I had one small paintbrush for the fine features, a medium paintbrush, and a large paintbrush to do the brunt of the work. I went back inside the shed to grab a blanket and another bucket to fill with water so I could wash my paintbrushes in between colors.

When I came back out of the shed, I looked back toward the fence and was very confused. Our fence has no doors on it so that no one can enter, but now there's a square door right where I was about to paint. You almost wouldn't notice it if there wasn't a large black doorknob attached to the left side of it. I stood outside the shed holding my blanket and bucket that has no water in it yet and look around confused. "No way was that there before", I thought. I slowly stepped towards the door. I could feel the grass prickling my feet as I walked along. I kept looking around in case someone jumped out at me. Maybe someone installed the door and had put the knob on last and my parents forgot to tell me about it? "No", I thought, "that still doesn't make sense. Mom and dad always leave me notes if someone is going to be coming in the house or doing any kind of work when I'm home".

I looked up and saw that the sun was shining bright like it was noon instead of four p.m. Normally at this time, the sun was low enough that it wasn't coming into the backyard at all. "This is weird..." I thought to myself. My heart started to beat a little faster which then started my anxiety going. "I'm going to be fine." I whispered to myself. I stopped walking and felt the cold earth under my feet. I took in a deep breath to calm down. I opened my eyes again and realized I was standing right in front of the door all of a sudden. I took another deep breath and reached for the black door knob. Oddly, the door was my exact height and only about four feet wide. I grabbed the door handle. It was as cold as ice. I let go due to the shock at the temperature of it. I looked around once more, bucked up my courage and grabbed the door knob again. Turning the knob felt like spreading butter on toast; it was so smooth. I stood there with the door wide open and looked through it. "Well that was anti-climatic", I said aloud to myself.

It's just the forest! Mom and dad must have had someone come and put in a door in the fence, and I missed them doing the work. That had to be the answer. I shrugged my shoulders and figured I'd just walk through anyways. I didn't bother to put shoes on either because I loved the feel of the earth. It reminds me that I'm alive from everything that I can feel. I noticed after I was about five feet from the door that the wind suddenly picked up. The sky was still clear so a storm shouldn't be coming. I looked around and noticed the door was now shut.

The wind must have shut it, no biggie. I thought. I stood still for a minute to enjoy the warm breeze flowing through my hair. I closed my eyes and took a deep breath. The smell of the forest never changes. The tree scent smells just like grass that's been freshly mowed and there's always a strong smell of dirt and humidity to go along with it. When I opened my eyes back up, I noticed there was something shining through the trees. It looked like it was coming from close to the ground and had to be a mile or so away. I stuck my toes in and out of the dirt while I pondered what it might be. I took a couple steps and noticed there was a sandy pathway to my right up ahead that looked like it led to the area that was shining. "How odd, I don't ever remember a sandy pathway being back here." I whispered to myself. "Maybe they did a whole landscaping job when they put the door in?" Since mom and dad wouldn't be home for awhile I figured it wouldn't hurt to go on a little adventure and see if I could find out what was glittering in the distance.

I walked up to the pathway and slowly put out one foot and put it in the sand. The sand was extremely soft under my foot. It was a pleasant surprise. I started walking at a slow pace, digging my heels into the sand as I walked along, looking around enjoying the nature. I noticed the birds were singing extra loud today. It was like listening to a symphony. A half hour went by and I started to worry if I should turn back. The glittering spot didn't look like it was getting any closer. What if I have an episode? I looked up at the sky and saw that I could still see the sun. Maybe I haven't been walking out here as long as I thought. I figure once the sun gets closer to disappearing is when i'll head back. After fifteen more minutes, I notice the shining spot is getting bigger. I pick up my pace from excitement. I want to run but I'm too scared it will make my heart beat uncontrollably. I control my breathing as the shining gets bigger and bigger. The willow trees are getting thicker and starting to surround the sand pathway. It starts to be completely shady as I have to keep moving the willow tree branches aside to keep going. At one point it was similar to pushing aside a thick veil. I kept going for another minute when the willow branches started getting thinner showing a lot of glittering through them. I must be close! I push the last veil of branches aside to reveal a large opening with a crystal blue lake in the middle. It's bright enough in this opening to make me think its noon again and not five pm. The sky is clear blue with a few puffy clouds. The lake is shining so brightly from what seems like the sun even though i can't see it. I take in another deep breath and notice the smell of the ocean. I am baffled yet intrigued at what I've found. "There's no way someone built all this in a day", I say aloud. I walk up to the lake and see a pasture full of flowers on the left side that come up to my waist. The right side of the lake looked like a freshly mowed lawn.

Even though I'm confused, I kept walking toward the lake. It looked so inviting. Maybe I'll just stick my feet in and wash them off and take a drink of water. I am thirsty after all, I've been out here for at least an hour. The sandy path breaches out to make a small beach that goes all around the lake. I dip my toe in the water to see how cold it is. It doesn't even feel like anything. The water must be the same temperature as the air. I go ahead and put both my feet in. It happened as soon as I put my feet in. My heart started beating out of control. I was having an episode. My heart speeds up to what feels like a million miles an hour. "Oh, no. What if I die here? Will anyone even be able to find me?", I thought with the fear building up inside me. I start to panic which makes my heart beat even faster. It feels like it's trying to break out of my chest. Tears gently roll down my face as I try to catch my breath. I'm so scared. It gets harder to breath as my vision starts to go black. The hyperventilation is starting except for the first time ever, my chest hurts too. It's like I swallowed a million bees and they are stinging me from the inside trying to get out. I grab my chest and close my eyes while the world starts to feel like its falling away from me. Then, out of nowhere, for the first time ever. Everything suddenly stopped. My episode disappeared and my breathing went back to normal. I felt... good. I slowly open my eyes and realized there's something underneath me. In between my legs was a dog looking up at me.

FOUR

A NEW FRIEND

The dog was as tall as my knees, had an all-black face and ears with a white nose and painted on brown eyebrows. It was looking up at me and leaning into my left leg. It was so cute but where did it come from and how did I not feel it come underneath me? It opened its mouth as if to smile at me and I felt it start to shake like it was wagging i's tail. Sure enough, I turned around and see an all brown tail wagging back and forth. I reach down to pet it and it reaches its head towards my hand. As I pet its head I notice how calm I feel. I can't remember the last time I felt this calm. I back out of the water because I notice it's starting to get cold. The dog stays where it's at. I get on the beach and sit down in the sand. I call the dog to me to see if it'll get out of the water. It turns around and slowly starts coming towards me. I notice it's a girl dog. I've never seen any other dog like her. She looks like she's not quite an adult dog but not a puppy either. She must be only a year old or so. Besides her face and tail, her whole torso is black and then her legs are fully brown with her paws being full black again. She prances toward me, with her pink tongue sticking out of her mouth looking as happy as a dog could ever be. I start to notice my anxiety coming back and get an instant rush of adrenaline. I start to tear up in the split second that I feel the anxiety. Scared that my heart was about to have another episode and worried that in case this dog isn't as friendly as she looks, that something terrible will happen to me. Before I could think anymore, she sat down right next to me and sat her head on my shoulder. Instant calm came over me again. I felt completely at peace. This was so strange but I was thankful she was here. I sat there for another ten minutes to make sure I was feeling ok and then slowly started to stand up. The dog stood up on all fours with me and looked up at me smiling. It was the kind of smile a mother would give her child. It was foreign, yet comforting to me. I suddenly felt very attached to her. "I'm going to see if mom and dad will let me keep you", I say to her. "Hi pretty girl, do you want to come home with me?" For a second, I thought she nodded back at me. She started wagging her tail excitedly and rubbed herself along my leg. "I think I should name you",

I said to her. "What about..." I drag out the word and pause for a minute trying to think of cute puppy names. She then sat on my foot and a name immediately popped in my head. Savior. "How about I call you Savior? Would you like that?" She gazed up and back at me from my foot with a smile of approval. "Ok, Savior it is. Let's go home, huh?". She got up off my foot and walked to the path before I got there. It's like she already knew the way to her new home. I let her walk in front of me and lead. She stopped to get some nice ear scratches every once awhile, but otherwise kept going. Somehow the sun was still up. I've lost track of what time it could possibly be. I'm pretty sure there's no way the sun should still be up though. I shrug my shoulders at this thought and my mind goes silent as I follow Savior on the path. For the first time in a long time, thoughts of my cardiac episodes weren't filling my mind. I felt peace and contentment just listening to the birds, and following my new dog home. Finally, I can see my fence. She walked up to the fence and sat down. *She is such a good dog for a stray* I think to myself. I grab the doorknob of the mysterious door and opened it. Savior went through first and then me. I walked through and everything instantly went dark. I was stunned, standing there barefoot in my grassy backyard. All of a sudden, it was night out. The full moon was right above me and the stars were out. *Something weird is going on* I thought. I turned around to shut the door but it was gone. The fence is completely whole again. I closed my eyes and took a deep breath in. The world once again, went dark.

When I opened my eyes, my parents were sprinting out of the back door towards me. Savior stepped from out in front of me and went to my left side instead opening a path for them. She leaned her head onto my leg. "Where have you been?!", Mom hysterically yelled at me. Dad grabs me and hugs me without saying a word. Mom starts crying. "We were so worried! Where did you go? It's midnight and your paint supplies were out by the fence but you were nowhere to be found. We even called the police to start a search party. Bill, go inside and call the search party off". Dad ran back into the house without saying a word to me. Mom hugs me too and then notices the dog beside me. She kissed me on the forehead and then took a step back. For some reason, my gut was telling me not to tell them what happened. It feels like a magical dream just happened and if I tell the truth, I'm afraid Savior will disappear. I looked down at Savior and then up at my mom. "I'm so sorry, mom". I was going to paint and then got distracted because I heard something behind the fence. When I went out into the forest to check what it was, I found this dog. I was gone for so long because it took me awhile to chase her down and get her to come to me. But then after I did she was super sweet and cuddly.

Can we keep her, please?". She looked at the dog and approached her. Savior didn't leave my side but wagged her tail and gave my mom the same smile she gave me. My mom looked a bit taken back at first but then went up to Savior and started petting her. "Well... I suppose if your father agrees, we can talk about keeping her." Just as she said that dad came walking out of the house. "They called off the search, Tracy. We have to go into the police station tomorrow to sign the report to close it out, but no harm done otherwise". He turned and looked at me and then the dog. Mom went up to him and quietly told him what had happened while I stood there with my hand on Savior's head. Dad looked displeased and concerned. Him and mom both walked up to Savior and checked her out. "Well", he grunted, "she seems friendly enough. We will put out a notice around the community that a stray was found, and if no one claims her within the next two weeks you can keep her". I let out a sigh of relief. I'm not worried anyone will claim her. I have a feeling she was meant for me. "Ok", i said as i smiled at them. "Go inside and get her a bowl of water and leave her out some meat from the refrigerator until we can go to the store tomorrow and pick her up some dog food." Mom stated as she pet Savior. I nodded and started walking into the house. Savior calmly followed without any prompting. I grabbed the door handle and opened it into the kitchen as Savior followed me in. She gladly accepted the water and lunchmeat that I left out for her. *I should probably shower before I get into bed,* I thought to myself as I started going upstairs to my bedroom. I looked down at my legs and feet and they were completely clean. How is this possible? I was in the forest all afternoon. You'd think my legs and feet would be dirty. It was like I never left the house. Considering how tired I was, I didn't fight the thought and just accepted that I was clean. I decided to sleep with my door closed in case Savior tried to go out and get into anything. I opened the door into my bedroom and waited for Savior to come in before closing the door. After she was in the room with me, I closed the door and grabbed an extra blanket out of my closet for her to sleep on. I put it at the end of my bed that way I didn't step on her when I got up in the morning. She curled right up and seemed to fall instantly asleep. I walked into the bathroom that connected to my room and undressed and brushed my teeth. I looked at my twin bed and felt comforted by seeing her laying at the end of it. I am not sure what happened this afternoon, but I'm thankful.

The next day was my cardiac appointment. I always hated going there because I'm scared of when I'll have to get surgery. I woke up in the morning less anxious than I usually was but still nervous. I slowly climbed out of my pink silk covers and put my feet on the floor. I rubbed my feet into the carpet to relax myself while I tried not to think about going to my appointment. I got up to get dressed and then remembered that Savior was here! I rushed to the end of my bed and saw that she was sitting there looking up at me, like she was just waiting for me to get ready. Her big brown eyes were full of reassurance that I was going to be ok. I got down on the blanket with her and gave her a big hug around her neck. "I am so glad I found you." I whispered to her as I hugged her. I stood up off the blanket and went to my dresser to get dressed. I always wore jeans and a flowy shirt when going because of the equipment they had to hook me up to. I try and look nice when I go out of the house because it makes me feel more normal like everyone else. I get to my bedroom door and see that Savior is waiting by the steps for me. I quickly go into the bathroom to brush my teeth and then head downstairs with her. Mom and dad already cooked breakfast for us before we had to leave. They always made a big breakfast to make the morning seem more fun. Today they made cherry crepes, scrambled eggs and waffles. It was delicious. We ended up feeding Savior some lunchmeat out of the fridge again. She ate it up gratefully and had some water. "Sweetie, do you have everything you need to go? Do you remember what you need to tell the doctor?" my mom asked. I told her yeah as I grabbed my backpack that had my medical journal in it. Whenever I had episodes, I wrote them down in this journal and gave it to the doctor at my appointments so he knew how far along my conditions progressed. We locked up Savior in the kitchen with access to the backyard before we left in case she tried to tear up things in the house. I gave her a pat and a kiss on the head and then followed mom and dad out the door. It's about an hour drive to my doctor, which I usually dread because it gives me way too much time to think about death and my condition, but today was different.

After I gave Savior a kiss on the head, I felt a wave of calm rush over me. The whole drive, I had no thoughts go through my head. I was completely at peace. Mom and dad talked in the front seat per usual about my condition and what they need to tell the doctor, but I paid no mind to it. I just stared out my window at the sky. We arrived and parked in the parking garage that belonged to the hospital. St. Johns Hospital is where my doctor resided. It was a huge city hospital an hour south of Theo. We decided to come here because of the genetic research they did with kids along with the great cardiac program they have. My doctor, Dr. Wayne Spellman was also known for being one of the best cardiologists in Ohio. He knew my parents from college where they all shared a love for genetics. After we parked, we went to the glass elevator in the parking garage that took us up to the 10th floor where my doctor was located. No one talked. Normally we were all in our heads, dreading the diagnosis from my doctor; but today was different for me. I was actually enjoying the view out of the elevator. The elevator made a loud ding as the doors opened up to reveal a large lobby that had four doctors' offices in it. Me and my dad went to the corner to sit down while mom went up to the receptionist to check us in. Since my doctor is so well known, sometimes we wait for three hours or more to see him. Today was no different. Dad and I goofed around and played with the games they had for the kids in the lobby while mom watched tv. They normally had on Soap Opera's or the History channel for adults on. As me and dad finished up another game of tic-tac-toe, the nurse called us back to the private rooms. She checked my vitals and then checked me into my room. Normally we had another hour in my room waiting, but dad only was able to spin me on the doctor's swivel chair a couple times before he walked in. I always enjoyed seeing Dr. Spellman even under sad circumstances. He had a southern accent and called me his sweet bell patient because he said I'm just always so sweet. He opened the door to the exam room and chuckled at me and my dad spinning in his chair. "I see my sweet bell patient is feeling well today, huh?" he said in his southern accent as his glasses slid down his large nose. He was shorter than my dad at about five-four and in his sixties, and was bald. He was a typical little southern man. I loved seeing him. He really made me feel special which was nice because I'm isolated normally. The nurse came in after him and talked to him about my vitals. He nodded his head and smiled at her as she handed him my chart and walked out. "I see your vitals are looking good today, how are you feeling?" he said to me. I explained that my episodes were getting worse and more frequent but that I hadn't had one today. I felt really good today. I handed him my journal and he flicked through it briefly.

His eyebrows furrowed as he got to the end. "Lay down on the table for me, I'm going to listen to your heart." he said after he put the journal down on the counter. He put the stethoscope to my chest. "Well, you're not having any palpitations and your heart rate sounds good. I can't even hear any dysfunction like usual". He sat me up and turned around to my parents and scheduled a couple of tests to look at my heart further to see how it looks from an inside perspective. My tests took another two hours and then we were finally done. It was an odd day. Mom and dad kept looking at me and asking me how I felt and I was actually honest when I said I was doing good. Mom rubbed my back as we got back into the glass elevator to go to the parking garage. My parents kept exchanging glances at each other the rest of the way home. I could tell they were uneasy and thought I wasn't being honest with them about how I was feeling. We walked in the door and Savior was laying in the middle of the backyard sleeping. Nothing was destroyed or out of place. I immediately set my backpack down and ran out into the backyard to snuggle Savior. She was smiling at me again. The sun made her seem so bright. I got down on my knees in the grass and put my arms around her neck for a big hug. She nuzzled right into me.

A week had passed since my appointment. I still hadn't had an episode and I was feeling better than I ever have. Savior officially was a part of our family. She had a dog bed in my room and her own food downstairs in the kitchen. Mom and dad even took a liking to her and would cook her fresh food along with ours for dinner some nights. Life was good. Eight days after my appointment my doctor called my mom with my test results. She took the call in the kitchen as she was cooking our dinner and stopped what she was doing. She sat down. For the first time in awhile, I felt my stomach drop. I wondered what the bad news was. Mom hung up the phone and started crying. She looked at me with concerned eyes as my dad came up to me and guided me to the kitchen table where she was sitting. I stood beside her and gave her a hug. I was too nervous to sit down. She grabbed my hand and said "Lily, this is amazing news. The doctor said a miracle happened. Your tests came back and your heart is completely healed. Somehow, someway... you no longer have a heart condition." I stood there confused. "How, though? I mean, I've been feeling fine, but how is this possible?", I asked her. Tears started rolling down my cheeks before I realized what I felt. Normally when I cried, I would go into an episode within thirty seconds. Yet, now my heart is reacting to it normally. It's still beating fine, so this must be true. Savior was by my leg wagging her tail looking up at me. I bent down and gave her a big hug. I held her while she nuzzled into my neck for awhile. I glanced up at my mom and dad and saw them hugging each other and calling some of my close family members. It's a miracle. I am finally free. I am going to live. Mom and dad came over to me and pulled me close. Savior even joined in on the family hug as we stood in the kitchen holding each other. It was the night that changed my life.

As I got ready for bed, I was still in shock. I can't believe I'm healed. How was this possible? I went into my room where Savior was sitting by my bed, waiting for me to get in. She's gotten in this habit where she lays her head on the bed by me until I fall asleep and then goes to her dog bed to go to sleep herself. I crawled into bed. Tonight she put her head on my chest. I put my hand on her head that's leaning on my chest and stroked her ears. Everything changed when she came along. It's been so surreal. The day I found her was strange, yet beautiful. I don't know what happened to me, but I'm grateful. "You know what, Savior. I think you were my heart healer." I said to her. She wagged her tail and licked me on my hand. Then for a second it was like she winked at me. I gave her another kiss on her head and scratched her head until I dozed off to sleep.

EPILOGUE

As Lily grew up, she continued to stay healed. Within a month of her cleared diagnosis, she was able to return to school. She was even allowed to bring Savior to school as she was registered as an emotional support dog. All the teachers loved Savior and the kids loved to play with her during recess and lunch time. Lily reunited with her friends and even made some new ones. As she grew up, she graduated high school and chose to follow her parents footsteps and go to college to study science. She focused on genetics and the cardiac system. By the time she was a junior in college, she found a passion and a determination to heal others hearts like hers was magically healed. After graduation she went to graduate school and worked in a research lab where she became a part of her own research. She tested her genetics and her blood to try and determine how she was healed. It turned out, her body was able to produce some new chemical that was able to heal organs in the human body. She was able to extract this chemical and developed a drug that other heart patients could take. She ended up winning the Nobel Prize for Science and went on to save millions of heart patients' lives. Savior, of course, was with her the whole time. Savior was in college with her and in her research laboratory as she performed her research and developed this miracle drug. Lily never married, but stayed in a small house she built outside of Theo with Savior. As she neared the end of her life, she stopped working and instead focused on writing her story down so that everyone knew about that magical day that happened to her. After all, she never did tell anyone how she found Savior. When Lily neared her late 90s, she finally finished her story. It was said that she passed away peacefully at ninety-eight. She was found by a younger doctor of hers that she had helped mentor some years ago. When they found Lily passed away peacefully in her bed, it was said that Savior had also passed away. When they were found, Savior was lying on Lily's torso with her head on her chest. They were embraced in hug. It was the life of Lily that forever changed the world, yet she always credited Savior for being the real heart healer.

ABOUT LORRAINE BRADNER

Lorraine Bradner, Author of 50 Ways to Be Petty, received their Masters Degree in Toxicology from the Michigan State University. Born on a farm in Ohio, Lorraine loved growing up in the country and playing outside. As an only child, Lorraine found friends in her books and one day dreamed of becoming an author. As a cardiac patient herself suffering from anxiety, Lorraine is no stranger to adversity and stressful events. Lorraine hopes to inspire others through her stories and bring comfort to those that may be struggling. When not writing, Lorraine enjoys going to the gym, watching movies, and of course, reading! Watch out for more from this young author as she is only just getting started in her writing career.